Seeing Lorna sitting there, cradling and rocking a baby, knocked the breath out of him.

She would have been a beautiful mother. Even now, with someone else's child, she fairly glowed. And the expression on her face as she talked to the child—or was she singing a lullaby?—that expression was as close to perfect contentment as he'd ever seen.

He tried not to think about it too often, about losing their child. Sometimes, though, in the empty moments, he still fantasized about what it would have been like being a father. At times he pictured himself as a father to a little boy, playing ball and all the games little boys liked to play. Then there were times when he was the father of a beautiful little girl. She looked like Lorna—same smile, same wide eyes. Then his heart broke, because that would never happen.

Did Lorna still think about it? Did her heart still break?

Sighing, he headed over to the food tent for a bitter cup of coffee, then wandered over to the supply tent to check the rescue grid and plot the next group out. As he passed by the hospital tent he didn't look in at Lorna, didn't look in at the child she still sat with. He couldn't. Not right now. Not while the fantasy of Lorna sitting next to the bed of *their* child, singing a gentle lullaby, was ripping at his heart.

Now that her children have left home, **Dianne Drake** is finally finding the time to do some of the things she adores—gardening, cooking, reading, shopping for antiques. Her absolute passion in life, however, is adopting abandoned and abused animals. Right now Dianne and her husband Joel have a little menagerie of three dogs and two cats, but that's always subject to change. A former symphony orchestra member, Dianne now attends the symphony as a spectator several times a month and, when time permits, takes in an occasional football, basketball or hockey game. Dianne loves to hear from readers, so feel free to e-mail her at DianneDrake@earthlink.net

Recent titles by the same author:

THE
RESCUE DOCTOR'S
BABY MIRACLE

BY
DIANNE DRAKE

MILLS & BOON®

First published in Great Britain 2007
Harlequin Mills & Boon Limited,
Eton House, 18-24 Paradise Road, Richmond, Surrey TW9 1SR

© Dianne Despain 2007

ISBN-13: 978 0 263 19795 2
ISBN-10:   0 263 19795 6

Set in Times Roman 10 on 12¼ pt
15-0307-58166

Printed and bound in Great Britain
by Antony Rowe Ltd, Chippenham, Wiltshire

THE
RESCUE DOCTOR'S
BABY MIRACLE

For Julie Rowe and Donnell Bell,
good friends who support me every step of the way.
Thanks for being there!

CHAPTER ONE

"WHY the hell did you say yes?" Dr Gideon Merrill slung the backpack over his shoulder and headed to the airplane door. It had been a long, bumpy flight in, he was moderately airsick from all the tossing and turbulence, and now this! He had half a mountain sliding down on top of a *favela*—house upon house built up the side of a mountain—more than twenty people reported missing, and who knew how many injured or dead. Two straight days of hard-hitting rain, and the river on the outskirts of town had burst its banks, flooding the streets down below with mud and water and debris washed down from the mountainside village. According to the weather experts, this little area of Brazil had been pounded by two months' worth of rain in two days. Six different neighborhoods had been washed out, and he had a keen suspicion that twenty people missing in all this was a hugely conservative estimate. Time and experience had taught him never to trust the first casualty estimates.

And if that wasn't enough, Lorna was coming. Of all the people in the world, Lorna! It wasn't like he didn't have enough headaches already, just getting the operation up and running. "Big headache, big pain in the…" he muttered.

Shoving a crate of shovels and other digging tools over to the door, Gideon's partner, Jason Getty, stopped just at the edge and looked down at Gideon. "I said yes because better exposure means more money, and more money means a new airplane, or at least a significant overhaul to the old one." A year younger than Gideon, who was thirty-six now, Dr Jason Getty was the polished edge to the rescue group, Global Response. He worried enough for the whole lot of them, but he kept them on the practical line, business-wise. He'd been Gideon's only choice as partner when the ownership title for the outfit had been transferred to him a year ago. Co-owners of an operation that didn't turn a profit...not very impressive on the résumé, or in the bank accounts. But it had its share of rewards. "And where are we going to get better publicity? Her name is pure gold, you know that! People love her. She's smart, she's sassy, and she's not bad on the eyes. A nice package all the way around, and on top of it, she's a doctor, so she understands why the need is so crucial. Pretty good deal for us, I'd say!"

"Pretty good deal? You didn't even have the decency to ask me before you let this...this TV medical guru come down," Gideon grumbled as he helped offload the crate of shovels. It wasn't raining at the moment, but this was December, and December in Brazil meant only one thing. More rain. "Or even mention that you were thinking about it."

"Get over it. Deal is done. She's on her way."

"And we can't have them turn the plane around?"

Jason scowled across the wooden crates at his partner. "When you took me on, it was as an equal partner. Equal all the time, Gideon. Not just when it suits you. And you specifically said you didn't want to be involved in any of the business aspects of the operation. This is a business aspect, so butt out! Lorna Preston is coming and there's nothing you can do about it."

"Except keep her the hell away from me." *Way the hell away*.

"Your choice. There are plenty of other people who will make a good story."

"From the perspective of a doctor who probably doesn't remember one end of the stethoscope from another." It was a waste of good medical talent, using it all on the telly, answering questions people should be asking their own doctors. None of his business, though. He practiced his medicine and she practiced hers.

"She's big time, buddy, whatever you think of her. When Lorna Preston wants to go with you to film a documentary, you'd have to be crazy to refuse her. I'm not crazy, and as far as I'm concerned, it's the opportunity of a lifetime. So, if you can't co-operate or get along, stay away. OK? I don't want your mood messing this up for us." He tossed a sack of alcohol swabs at Gideon. "And you're so damned crabby, you will."

"Fine! I'll stay away from her. No big deal." he said, defen-sively. As far away as he could.

"I mean it, Gideon," Jason warned. "I don't know what it is about Lorna Preston that sets you off, but I worked hard to get her here and I don't want you so much as looking cross-eyed at her!"

Point taken. Lorna Preston, or as she'd once been called, Lorna Preston Merrill, was valuable to them. He'd put his feelings aside because of that. Simple enough. Except, there was nothing simple about his feelings for her. Yes, she was the op-portunity of a lifetime for them right now, but he'd thought along those same lines seven years ago, when they'd pronounced their marriage vows. Not that the marriage had gone very far.

Gideon huffed out an impatient sigh. Now wasn't the right time to tell his partner that an ex-wife didn't make the best tag-along, when the partner didn't even know there'd been an ex-wife in his past. "Well, since it's a done deal, I'll be good. No cross-eyed looks…"

"No cross words."

Jason had no idea what he was asking. Cross words were just about the only thing he remembered from their marriage. Cross words, and their baby. "No cross words. But I'm warning you.

Jason, we don't have time to deal with her since we're already short-staffed on this trip. She's on her own. No one gets assigned to escort her, wait on her, or pamper her the way she's used to being pampered. She's here at her own risk and she gets nothing from us other than the story she's after."

"Fine."

"No special privileges, and if she gets in the way—"

"Fine!" Jason snapped before Gideon was even through speaking. "I get it. We'll keep her on a short leash. One shorter than we keep the dogs on. Does that make you happy?"

Gideon shook his head, and finally conceded a smile. "For what it's worth, I think you're right. The publicity will do us some good. Every time we get called out it seems the resources get tighter and tighter, so a little attention from Lorn..." Lorn, his pet name for her. She was already intruding and she wasn't even here. "A little attention from Lorna Preston can't hurt."

"If that's an apology, I'll accept it," Jason responded, finally sounding a little less tense.

Gideon nodded. Jason might be right about this, but that didn't mean he had to like it. Global Response was suffering, however. Never enough supplies and equipment to go around. This time they simply didn't have the resources to haul in everything they needed, given the rescue operation they were about to start. They'd had to go shy on bringing in a full crew of medics and rescue workers in order to get all the medical and rescue equipment in, because they didn't have the means to bring along an abundance of both. So, it all boiled down to pick and choose. Which wasn't acceptable for a rescue response, even though it was the best they could do. "Yeah, it's an apology," he said, and meant it. Jason's idea to draw attention to their work was brilliant. But, damn it, this was Lorna. Of all the journalists in the world, why her?

"She's promised to stay out of the way. Do her filming on the sidelines, and respect any rules we lay down for her. She understands what we're dealing with and, in my opinion, it doesn't get more co-operative than that."

Co-operative maybe, but his definition of *out of the way* for Lorna was a swank hotel all the way up in Rio. Better yet, back in the States. Unless she'd had some kind of major life change, Lorna simply wasn't suited for this kind of a rescue operation. Never had been. She was spoiled, pampered. Couldn't step out of the house without her make-up. And, yes, animosities aside, he'd watched her make her way, these past years, as a media medical expert. Call it curiosity, call it nostalgia, call it anything you liked, but he'd been glued to her career. *Ask Dr Lorna* was her daily five-minute segment on the national morning news program, where people called in or e-mailed with health questions. Then there were the health documentaries she produced, and books and articles she'd written.

OK, he'd admit it. He was a little impressed by it all. When they'd started their marriage all she'd wanted was a traditional practice. At least, that's what she'd said. And he'd liked that. But by the time they'd ended, she had been well on her way to being Ask Dr Lorna. They'd never discussed it, she'd never even mentioned she had been thinking of taking her career in a different direction. One day out of the blue, only a month after they'd taken their marriage vows, she'd casually mentioned that an unusual opportunity had come up. One of her patients, a television producer, had made her an offer...

Just like that, his wife had become a journalist. His wife, his parents...his upbringing had always been a bit of an uproar, with both parents being journalists who never knew where their next assignment would take them. Living that way throughout his childhood had been one thing, but it certainly hadn't been what he'd expected in his marriage.

He remembered the way his young life had always been on

the edge. It had been a hard lesson learnt then, not to count on anything. Which was why, when he'd met Lorna and she had been on the path of something traditional, he'd thought he'd found heaven.

But then she'd brought hell to their relationship with a simple announcement, and hadn't even had to decency to discuss it with him before she'd taken the job.

Then when she'd said she was bringing a baby into it…

Well, apparently Lorna's life was working well for her, because she was a huge success now. He didn't begrudge her that, but he *did* begrudge her tagging along on a rescue operation where she had no business being, especially since he knew her true tendencies. "I trust you to make sure she does know her place. And, Jason, I don't want to have cameras in my face every time I turn around. The people here deserve some respect and privacy, and they're not going to get that with *Miss* Preston tramping around all over them. Make sure she understands that she's to allow them their privacy."

"Hey, don't worry about it. OK? She's not exactly an amateur in these matters, and she's promised to run everything she films by us before it goes out to the public. Nothing intrusive is going to slip by. Personal guarantee." He crossed his heart, grinning.

"Well, gee. Now I feel better." Gideon pulled a case of first-aid supplies out the airplane door as Jason shoved a crate of blankets and clothes at him.

"If I didn't know better, Gideon, I'd say you're sounding like a man who has a grudge against the lady. Since I know for a fact that you live the life of a monk…"

"Knock it off," Gideon chided. "No grudges here." A few raw, unresolved feelings maybe, but no grudge.

"Gideon!" Danica Fielding called from across the encampment. "Max, Philo and Dag are out of the crates. We're going to take them for a walk, let them have some exercise, get them acclimatised to the area." Danica, or Dani, as she was called, was the resident veterinarian for Global Response, the one who went along to take care of the rescue dogs. On top of that, she was a top-notch paramedic, a real gem in the medical field with enough optimism to lift the spirits of the entire medical unit even under the most discouraging circumstances. More than any of his other crew, Dani was a breath of fresh air. "Max is doing fine," she said reassuringly, as she attached a lead to the dog's collar. "Do you want to walk him?"

Quickly, Gideon glanced over his shoulder to find Max. The dog fared—these trips better than *he* did, but he always fretted over him like a protective father would. Rescue dogs were an important part of the effort, and their contribution in finding victims could never be diminished. In short, the dogs saved lives, too. All that aside, he simply loved his dog. Call it mushy, call it impractical. Max was his family. His only family. "Go on ahead," he called. "I've got Priscilla and Harry already on their way to set up a base camp, and Brian and Gwen are making contact with the local authorities already, trying to get the volunteers in place. So you and Tom take the dogs on down that way, and we'll join you as fast as we can get the gear loaded up." Tom, a registered nurse, and Dani, were on the verge of being a couple. The signs were all there, and it was only a matter of getting them into the right position, somewhere far, far away from a rescue scene.

Gideon hoped that when it happened they would have better luck at it than he'd had with Lorna.

He glanced out over the supplies, and to the people emerging from nowhere who were already loading them into the transport truck supplied by the local authorities. This was the part that never ceased to amaze him. Ten minutes on the ground and they were already on the move. All the regular rescue workers knew their roles, and no one had to be told what to do once they went into rescue mode. It was like a well-oiled machine—three doctors, three nurses, two paramedics, and four general volunteers who did everything but the medical work. Plus dozens of volunteers from the local areas. It was such a vast wealth of talent that came together on virtually a moment's notice, and he wasn't in the mood to disrupt it with his ex-wife. Or maybe he wasn't in the mood to disrupt himself with his ex-wife. "When do you expect her ?" he asked Jason, who was pulling the last crate of supplies out of the airplane.

"Why do you care?" Jason asked. "Because, with your attitude, I'm not letting her within a mile of you!"

"Don't care," he snapped. "Just curious."

Jason paused, giving his partner a curious look. "You need a holiday. You're getting too grouchy. When this one is over, you're taking a week off, like it or not. By order of *this* boss! And if you so much as utter one word of complaint, I'm making that two weeks, mandatory."

Gideon bit back his protest. No use going against Jason. Especially when Jason was as right about this as he was about bringing Lorna there. It had been years since he'd taken more than a day off, and having Lorna here shouldn't cause him to be so grumpy. He was tired, though. Down-to-the-bone tired. That's why he was over the top about her. Had to be it. Just tired, that's all. "Keep backing," he called to the transport driver. "A little more…keep coming…a little more… Stop!"

Gideon and Jason picked up the first of the folded tents and flung it into the back. "I'll consider the holiday, and I won't say another word against Miss Preston. But like I said—"

"I know what you said, and if you want my opinion, you'll take that holiday and go somewhere with lots of women and re-acquaint yourself with the very finest things in life!"

After the two of them had slung several more tents into the transport, Jason hopped up in the back of the drab green, tarp-covered truck to shove the crates to the front to make more room for the remaining supplies. "I've looked," Gideon growled. "And dated. Don't need to reacquaint myself with anything."

"If you've looked and dated, it's not so anyone would notice."

Oh, I've noticed, Gideon thought as he grabbed up the first crate of kitchen supplies to sling into the transport. He'd definitely noticed. Mostly Lorna. Always on the telly.

Unfortunately, any other notice of anyone else simply hadn't stacked up.

Francisco do Monte. When she'd learned they were going to a village on the edge of a Brazilian jungle, this hadn't been what she'd expected. Somehow, she'd had images of thatch-roofed huts, and genial natives, and children playing among the palms, being observed by the wary *capivara*, or shooing off a basking red-necked *tuiuiú*. But she'd flown into Rio de Janeiro, a beautiful city barely inconvenienced by the rains, and traveled south in a truck leant to her by one of the television stations to this. It wasn't quaint, and it wasn't a village in any way she defined one. It was a washout, a gully of mud and water, and houses slid down from their precarious perches on the mountain and crashed into the houses just below them. House heaped upon house, like pancakes in a stack.

And so much mud. Dear God, this wasn't at all the village trek she'd been expecting.

Lorna Preston climbed out of the truck that had brought her halfway from the helicopter, grabbed her overnight bag and make-up case, and immediately sank up to her ankles in the mud. But instead of fighting her way back out of it, she simply stood there and stared at everything surrounding her, trying to make sense of it all. Mud-caked people were everywhere—running, walking. Some carrying children, some carrying personal objects—big baskets and bundles of a life's possessions. Some were helping the elderly while others were simply trying to make it on their own.

Everywhere around her the screams of babies cut through the other noises, while the barking of dogs being coaxed along with their owners was almost as loud as the babies. People were working hard to get through the mud and the congested knot of other people—people trying to get away from Francisco do Monte just like everybody else. But no one was panicked. Some actually smiled, others laughed. It was like the blow life had dealt them wasn't as great as their resilience. Such an amazing thing to witness, and while she'd initially complained about coming here, especially when she'd found out about Gideon, she was already glad she had. This was going to make a great story.

"Frayne," she called to her cameraman. "Are you getting any of this?"

She turned around to see if he had his camera going, but he was already out of the truck, making his way through the hordes of people. There probably wasn't much that Jim Frayne, a veteran of world disasters and wars, hadn't seen, but for Lorna this was a first. As a doctor, she'd witnessed firsthand the worst of human suffering, but always in a contained setting. In the hospital, in the emergency department, at a patient's bedside. Never anything in the up close and personal sense like this was. Somehow, on television, which was her narrow view of the world, it always looked different. Buffered, maybe. Or from a wide-angle shot to spread it out. But here…this wasn't spread out, and nothing was buffered.

It was a mix of tragedy and spirit and the sheer determination to hold on. For her, if nothing else, this first glimpse was humbling.

So, was *he* here yet? When she'd learned that her producer was hooking her up with her ex-husband, she'd begged off the assignment, asked to turn it over to someone else or drop it altogether. Five years between them now, and she was nervous. For the life of her, she couldn't imagine what would have possessed him to propose a rescue effort as a documentary filmed by her?

There were others who could have done it justice, others who wouldn't have come here fighting it like she had. Others who hadn't walked out on him and dragged him through a divorce the way she had.

Had Gideon finally gone round the bend? Had he forgotten their two-year try at married life, or had be decided there hadn't been enough of it to matter? Whatever the case, filming this rescue as a documentary was a brilliant idea. Filming it with Gideon a miserable one because there were two things she always stayed away from…chocolates and her ex-husband. Both gave her an excruciating headache.

"This way!" Frayne called. "They're setting up their base camp in the clearing on the knoll down at the bottom of the hill, and I'm going on ahead to start shooting it from the beginning."

"I'm right behind you!" And to think, this time yesterday she'd made plans for a day off. Her first one in months. Between her duties as an on-air medical consultant five days a week, and her medical duties as a regular consultant and teacher at Newport General Hospital just outside New York City, she barely had time to sleep. So she'd planned this day as a treat for herself. A little shopping, an hour at the spa, indulging in an absurdly expensive lunch with Lucy Bergen, her best friend ever since the divorce—yes, all that had been in the planning stages yesterday. Then today, here she was! Ankle deep in mud, and soon to be up to her knees.

And on her way to see Gideon.

Between the two, she wasn't sure which was the worst—Gideon, or the mud.

Sighing, Lorna looked down at the ground. Mud washed off easily. Gideon didn't. Even after five years away from him, there was a little bit of him still sticking to her somewhere.

The grueling trudge down the hill took longer than Lorna expected. She was fighting against the flow of a mass exodus, trying to tote her two bags, and people were none too observant of the crazy American woman oozing her way into the place they all wanted to leave. Several times she was knocked flat into the mud, and she was forced to push herself up against the odds. And several times she succeeded, only to be shoved back in. People were nice about it. They always stopped to help her to her feet, but that didn't change the fact that she seemed to be down more than she was up. "And to think I was actually going to pay for a mud bath at the spa today," she muttered, accepting the hand of a stranger as she forced her way back up for the fifth time in a dozen minutes.

"*Obrigado*," she said, as she made it to her feet. *Thank you.* One of the dozen or so Brazilian Portugese phrases she'd had time to learn on the trip down.

"Is that your lipstick?" the man said, pointing to the cosmetics that had spilled out of the case.

She wiped away the mud from her eyes with the muddy back of her hand, and looked up at her ex-husband. "Well, I thought of a lot of things to say at our first meeting, but I didn't expect it to be like this."

"I thought of a lot of things not to say," he retorted.

"So is this where we make nice, ask each other how we've been, what we've been doing with our lives, and pretend to be civil?" She squatted to retrieve her lipstick and foundation make-up and stashed them back into her case. Then she handed it up to Gideon, while she pulled her overnight bag from the mud.

"This is where I go back to base camp and you keep up with me if you can." He handed the bag back to her.

She studied him for a moment, head to toe, most of it covered in mud. "So tell me, Gideon, what am I getting myself into here?"

"Nothing you're going to like, Lorna."

Gideon might have been more handsome than she remembered. All the brief television clips she'd seen of him told her he was. Some people withered with age, some improved. Some exploded with good looks, and according to the last rescue clip of him she'd watched, Gideon had exploded. "Well, I'll admit, I was surprised when you asked for me…"

"For the record, my partner asked. I objected. He won because we need your publicity. So don't go getting some stupid notion that this is our reunion, because it's not, Lorna. We have a need which you can fulfill. If anybody could have done it better, they'd be here instead of you."

"Always the practical one, weren't you? Practical and not polite. Now, that's the old Gideon I remember."

"At least people know where I stand. No surprises."

Not even two minutes in, and they were right back where they had been five years ago when they'd signed the final decree officially ending their legal misery. "Where you stand, and from where you never, ever move." But what did she expect? A miracle transformation? A warm embrace at their first meeting? This was Gideon, after all, and Gideon was…Gideon. Except he was leaner now. More fit. Even in the muddy cover he wasn't much like the Gideon she remembered. That one was OK, this one was…better?

Instead of responding, Gideon turned and prepared to start down the trail. Lorna prepared to follow, but she'd taken only one step when she tripped over a tree branch sticking out of the mud and immediately started her spin back down to the ground. Gideon grabbed her, though, breaking her fall. And for that split second when he held on, a slight spark broke from the mud and sizzled all the way up the arm he held onto. She felt it, felt the pause in her thinking, felt an instant of confusion before she regained enough sense to break away from him, effectively short-circuiting the moment and the mood. "Thank you," she mumbled, uncharacteristically shaken. Just tired, she reasoned. Tired and overwhelmed by everything going on around her. That's all it was. All it could be.

"From here, it only gets worse," he quipped.

"I take it you're referring to the conditions. Not the great chasm between us."

"The chasm can't get worse. The physical conditions here can." Without asking, he took her overnight bag in one hand, then took hold of Lorna's arm in the other, practically pulling her through a cluster of people and donkeys making their way up the hill.

At the bottom of the hill, where the masses of people had thinned out, Lorna pulled out of Gideon's grasp and simply stopped to take a good look around. Beautiful area, overall. At least, without all the mud and destruction it would have been. "Why were you the ones called out?" she asked Gideon.

"Because we have not only the search-and-rescue capabilities, we also set up a hospital of sorts, since half our volunteers are medical. They needed someone with both those capabilities in here because it's a small enclosed area and transporting the people out is difficult. Plus Texas is in relatively close proximity to Brazil as rescue teams go." He waved at a man who was carrying an armload of blankets from one tent to another, and as the man saw them, he gave the blankets to yet someone else and hurried over.

"My partner," Gideon explained, then turned his back to answer his two-way radio.

"Some people call me the co-owner, but the only reason they want me is because I own the airplane that gets them where they need to go." The man stuck out his hand in greeting, grinning sheepishly when he saw how muddy it was. "My name's Jason Getty."

"And I'm—"

"I know who you are, ma'am. My wife watches you every morning, and swears by your health advice more than she does mine."

"You're a doctor?" Lorna asked.

"Yes, when I'm not a pilot." He took hold of her arm and

pulled her away from Gideon, who was still involved with someone on the other end of his radio. "We've already got volunteers out on the search, and casualties should start rolling in any time. So, take a look around. Get your bearings. Ask questions now, because when things pick up, we won't have time to answer." He glanced up at the sky, frowning. "We've got a storm coming in, and it's going to get crazy, especially if we have another section of the mountain wash down."

"How about I just observe for a while? My cameraman is off getting some background footage, so unless you have something specific in mind, let me walk around and see what's here. OK?" She glanced back at Gideon, who hadn't noticed in the least that she'd been pulled away from him. Just like when they'd been married.

"Sounds OK to me." He pointed to the two tents straight ahead. "Hospital tents. And the one adjacent is for supplies. That's the strategy center, too. Normally, we search by the grid, don't go out without a plan unless it's an emergency. So everything is plotted and planned in there. Over there, the food tent. We try to keep food and coffee going all the time."

"And you've set this up in how long?"

He glanced at his watch, even though the crystal was covered with mud. "A couple of hours now."

"And you're ready to go?"

Jason grinned. "We're never ready to go. We just do what we need to when we have time. Pretty much it's always something we don't expect."

Something they didn't expect... She knew all about that. Gideon had taught her well. One week out of the hospital and still so vulnerable and hurt over losing her baby that all she'd wanted to do had been to curl up in a fetal ball and die, she'd never expected Gideon to trot himself off to an emergency field services symposium. Which is exactly what he had done. But by that point in their marriage, she shouldn't have been surprised.

Perhaps the biggest surprise was that she had been surprised by him leaving her then. "How many patients can you handle?" she asked, trying not to think about the past.

"Forty comfortably. Fifty's a stretch but we manage. Sixty's a problem but we can work it out. More than that…" He shrugged, heading off to the hospital tent, gesturing for her to follow. "We do what we can."

"And how many people do you have to work the rescue?" Lorna asked, following.

"This callout is a dozen. We've taken as many as twenty, but we had too much weight to carry down this trip since the area isn't equipped with anything. You know…generators, supplies…We had to carry it all in. But sometimes we're lucky and get called out to an area that's already been set up by another group and we can share some of the basics. We weren't so lucky this time. Space is too limited, which meant we had to sacrifice volunteers for equipment."

"You're the only search-and-rescue group to come in?" she asked, quite amazed by that fact.

"In this spot, yes. There are others further north, but we've got about all the high ground there is to be found right here, so pretty much the whole face of the mountain on this side is ours to search."

Amazing. Impressive. So few people had already done so much. This story was getting better and better. "And you're all volunteers?"

"Everyone but Gideon. We need someone to co-ordinate and be on call twenty-four seven, and he's the one. The rest of us have day jobs."

"So this is how Gideon makes a living? He's not a practicing surgeon?" That was a surprise. When they'd been married, he had been a surgeon who'd volunteered occasionally with a rescue outfit. She hadn't known he'd made the change.

Jason chuckled. "If you want to call it a living. Let's just say it's a good thing he's a man of few needs."

He'd been in a lucrative medical practice. Showed lots of promise. And now Gideon was a man of few needs? She was still a little surprised by that. He'd had so many dreams and expectations for his surgical practice. "So, is your wife a doctor, too?"

"No. She's an accountant. But she comes out with us as a general volunteer. And she has a rescue dog."

"Then you don't have children?"

"We have two, and they're always glad to go off to Grandma's house when Mom and Dad have to go rescue someone."

He talked as if this was merely a casual way to spend a few days. Send the kiddies to Grandma, then go to a mudslide, a tsunami or an earthquake. "Your partner…Gideon…is he married, too?" Honestly, she didn't know. She'd taken a quick check of his left hand for a ring, but all she'd seen had been mud.

Jason barked out a sharp laugh. "Gideon, married? Not a chance in hell. It's just him and Max, and God help the woman who tries to come between them."

"Max?" she asked, almost too shocked to say the name. Gideon had ended up with someone named Max?

"His best friend, partner…got him as a pup, and spent two years training him. I'll swear the man lets him sit at the dinner table. Although he won't admit it."

"He's a dog," she said, actually relieved over that.

"Not just a dog. He's the best we've got on the team, although don't tell my wife I said that because she'll tell you her dog is the best." Jason waved to someone at the foot of the hill, a pretty blond woman Lorna took to be his wife, judging from the look on his face as he waved. "Look, I've got to get to work. Have a look around. Grab yourself something to eat if you're hungry. And stay out of Gideon's way."

"His rule?"

Jason nodded. "He's busy. Doesn't like being bothered."

By anybody? she wondered. Or just by her?

"If you need me, I'll be covering the critical injuries in the other tent." With that, he left her there as he trotted off to join the blonde. Standing in the mud, wondering what to do, Lorna was on her own. She took a wide turn to look for Gideon, and didn't see him anywhere. But why should she be surprised? This was the way she'd spent those last months of their marriage. Always looking, and always alone.

CHAPTER TWO

WELL, it wasn't what she'd expected. Lorna wasn't sure exactly what she'd thought she would find in the base camp hospital, but whatever kind of tidy arrangement she'd assumed she would discover, this wasn't it. For that matter, wasn't anything like it. On the bright side, there were floors—temporary sheets of plywood and odd planks thrown down over the muddy ground. And the tents were enclosed with mesh screens. They were erected straight into the mud and sagging against the wind, but they weren't collapsing. Inside the makeshift quarters were several cots, but twice as many beds were being set up on the floor. At first glace, Lorna saw that only the most elderly or badly injured were being given a bed off the ground. The others were made comfortable in blankets piled atop the splintery wood.

The jagged, stitched edges of a patched a hole in the screen mesh siding of the hospital caught her attention. There were several such patches. The top of the tent was patched, too. A large piece of brown canvas sewn over the green. She'd always known Gideon had worked under rough conditions when he'd gone out on a rescue, but somehow, she'd never imagined this. What she saw was medicine reduced to the barest elements. Wincing, she thought back to just last week when she'd mentioned to her hospital administrator that her office needed a fresh coat of paint.

The faded yellow of her walls compared to all this...Lorna winced again.

And the medical supplies... The only word she could think of to describe them was *meager*. Her first assessment saw the basics, enough to get the job started but not enough to finish it...set-ups for IVs, first-aid supplies such as gauze and tape. One corner of the tent was piled with crates marked 'splints and other orthopaedic equipment', while in another corner was piled identical crates only with the label of 'surgical'. It was such a jumble. Gideon's people had come in, they'd pitched it up as fast they could, and gone off on the rescue. The three dozen or so casualties already brought in were being treated by people who worked methodically to get everything done. "This is it?" she asked one of the volunteers who was running through with a portable oxygen set-up.

"This is it," said a large-boned nurse who didn't stop to introduce herself. "Probably not the image you were hoping to capture for your camera, is it?" she called back.

"Never mind her," a pudgy, curly-haired young man said, stepping up behind Lorna. "Gwen's good, with a huge heart, but she's strictly business. And I think she's a little put out having you here." He introduced himself as Monty Ward, one of the general volunteers. "Not medical," he said. "I run a delivery service in Houston."

"She's put out by me?"

"Not you so much as your cameraman. She's already kicked him out of the hospital tent. Said he was getting in her way." He smiled. "Don't take it personally. She's a little brusque at times, but always good at what she does."

Good at what she did but not so accepting of Lorna's presence. Fair enough. From now on, she'd make a point of staying out of Gwen's way, as well as Gideon's. "How many casualties do you expect in?" Lorna asked him.

"Last mudslide they had like this killed thirty-six people and injured a couple hundred," he called over her shoulder on his way out the door. "This one's not as bad so far. More people got out before the worst of it so I don't really have a clue"

Lorna shivered, thinking about treating so many people under these conditions. It was so bare, so stark. But then, in the research notes she'd read on the way down, the hospital operated on a revolving-door system. In and out as quickly as possible. Stabilize the patients, do the most necessary of emergency procedures then ship them to a real hospital so the next round of emergencies would have room. First-aid, on a little larger scale. No welcome mat, vases of flowers, or lingering.

That was basic!

Dropping her duffle onto one of the crates marked 'orthopaedic', Lorna pulled out a notepad then wandered up the central aisle, taking a quick look over the patients already bedded. No one seemed in distress. No one in immediate need, except the patient being set up with oxygen. Although she wasn't there in a medical capacity, those instincts came first. So she didn't start taking notes until her trip back down the aisle—notes for story ideas such as following one patient through from beginning to end, or concentrating on the work of one individual…such as Gideon. Which, of course, he wouldn't permit. But it was a thought.

It was an amazing sight, watching everybody work. No questions, very little communication. People came in and out, did what was necessary, didn't ask for direction. She did have to admit, from the little she'd seen so far, Gideon's people responded well. They got lots of credit for that. He got credit, too, for the training, for choosing the right people. It was hard imagining Gideon in the role of administrator, not the Gideon she knew, anyway. But something told her the old Gideon and the one who existed now were miles apart.

She thought about going to find Gideon and watching him for a while, but she wasn't ready, yet, to see him. So she simply picked up a stethoscope and set about taking vital signs. Seemed a logical thing to do. Gwen, the nurse, had more than she could handle at the moment, so why not? Blood-pressure, heart rates, pulse—all easy enough. So for the next hour, Lorna poked and prodded half the patients in her tent, as Gwen did the same with the other half. Then after that Lorna re-dressed a couple of wounds, did half a dozen neuro checks and toted water as well as a few bedpans. Patient care at the very roots. Admittedly, it felt good. In her part-time capacity as a consultant in the hospital, that's all she did—consult. Half the time was taken up with the paperwork associated with the patient and not patient care itself. And even when her duties involved patient care it was always so indirect she could have phoned it in.

So this felt good. It had been a long time since she'd stretched her medical muscles and, surprisingly, she realized she missed it.

"Not so bad," she said to herself, meaning the medical duty, as she elevated the leg of one patient assessed to have a bad sprain, but not a break. He didn't understand English, naturally, but he grinned at her anyway, glad of the attention. Lorna smiled back at him. "And it looks like you're going to be one of the lucky ones. By tomorrow you'll be ready to go home…" If he had a home. She gave him the thumbs-up sign and started across the aisle to give the patient a drink of water and a mild pain pill when two men toting a stretcher came straight through the central area and stopped in front of her, awaiting further instruction, like she was in charge.

One quick look at the man stretched out under the sheet, even though she wasn't really working there, told her more than she wanted to know. His leg was horribly damaged—so badly mangled her immediate reaction was to prescribe amputation in order to save his life. If she were prescribing anything medical here, which she wasn't. "Do you have a surgeon here?" she called to Gwen, who was in a frenzy over a patient in the throes of an epileptic seizure.

"Why?" Gideon asked, rushing in with phenobarbital for Gwen's patient.

She glanced over at him. Yes, he'd served a surgical residency, just like she'd served one in internal medicine. And for a time he'd even worked as a surgeon, fitting in his rescue callouts as permitted. She imagined he was still brilliant in surgery, the way he was then, because Gideon had never done anything that wasn't brilliant. "Because he needs a BK amputation, stat, and I'm an internist. I don't operate."

"You don't practice medicine here either," he said roughly.

"And you've got enough people you can refuse my help?" She did a quick blood-pressure check of the patient with leg injury, then looked over at Gideon. "Dropping. So now tell me, what do you use as an operating theater and who do you use as a surgeon?"

He pointed to a separate area curtained off at the end of the tent and gestured for the volunteers to take the man on in. "You don't have the temperament," he said to Lorna, as he followed the two attendants in.

She followed him through the curtains, then helped lift the patient over onto a portable operating table. "For what? Medicine? In case you're forgetting, I do have a medical license."

"You talk medicine, Lorna. Not practice it."

"I have a post at the hospital," she defended, whilst taking yet another blood-pressure check on the man.

"Doing what?"

"Working as a hospitalist. Seeing to the continuity of care between services." When one patient had more than one doctor, her job was to make sure the two medical practices lined up, that drugs or treatments prescribed by both didn't conflict or overlap.

In other words, she was the medical intermediary who made sure both medical services worked together. And a lot of that was…talk.

"Point made, Lorna," he said. "You talk." Grabbing a disposable surgical gown from an unpacked crate, he took one out for Lorna, too, and handed it over. "Now, start the IV for the anesthesia, then scrub up."

"So now you want me?"

"Not a matter of wanting so much as—"

"Needing me?" A smile slid across her face. "Point made, Gideon. Now, show me where I can find the IV set-ups."

Ten minutes later, the IV was inserted and Lorna was standing next to Gideon at a portable trough, scrubbing. "Any special instructions?" she asked.

"Nothing special. We try to keep everything simple around here."

"Well, simple I can handle," she said, giving a quick sideways glace at Gideon. Dressed in hiking boots, with a green gown tied loosely over his cargo shorts and T-shirt, and a paper cap over his shaggy brown hair, he looked more the mad scientist than the brilliant surgeon. But he was brilliant. Back in the day when all else had been breaking down around them, she'd always given Gideon his due. He was an amazing physician and an outstanding surgeon, even if his boots were now muddy.

"Can you use ketamine?" he asked Lorna. "Or have you used it?"

She blinked her surprise. "You don't have an anesthesiologist?" She was prepared to assist…hand him instruments, suction and suture the patient if that was required of her…but not administer anesthesia.

"Other than you, no. I have a veterinarian who usually does the duty because she uses anesthesia in her veterinary practice, making her more trained in it than any one else we've got, but she's out in the field. We can't wait for her to get back in. So you can do the amputation or the anesthesia, take your pick."

A cold chill ran over Lorna as she stepped over to the patient's bedside and looked down at him. He was young, probably not more than thirty. Unconscious from all the blood loss and barely clinging to life, all he had was the two of them to save that life. Gideon would operate, of course. No choice to be made there. But to leave her to do the rest? She shook her head skeptically. "Except for a short stint in anesthesia when I was an intern, I haven't…" This was such an odd place to be, especially since she was in it with Gideon. In all their time together they'd never worked with each other. In fact, professionally, their medical paths had never crossed except in the cafeteria at the hospital. And now…" Look, Gideon, I'll be honest. This scares the hell out of me."

"You were good, Lorna. Before you…"

She knew the rest of that even though he didn't say it. Before she'd turned her medical practice into television medicine. He'd taken it as a personal betrayal of some sort and he'd never forgiven her for that. Looking back, the day she'd told him she'd agreed to do a once-weekly medical segment on the local news had been the beginning of the end. The miscarriage had been the end. "I'm still good, Gideon. Maybe not by your standards, but by most others."

He gave her an odd look, a frown, but one more contemplative than angry or disapproving. "I'll talk you through," he said. "You'll do fine."

Lorna nodded as she took her place at the patient's head and awaited further instruction.

Gideon waited until she was settled, and had made sure the IV drip was adjusted accordingly and the oxygen was flowing. Then he began. "First, we won't intubate," he said. In other words, this was an injected anesthetic, not one administered through ventilation. "And what I need you to do is monitor his vitals and act as my surgical tech." He pulled his mask up over his nose then put on a pair of goggles.

"This wasn't what I had in mind when I came here," she said, pulling up her own mask and putting on her own goggles.

"It's never what I have in mind when I arrive," he said, "but you do what you have to do. Around here, we work from minute to minute and try not to think ahead of the moment. It keeps you focused, keeps you on the edge, which is where you need to be to get along." After snapping on his gloves, Gideon stepped back to appraise the wound, holding his gloved hands slightly away from the sides of his body in order not to contaminate them. "Oh, and just so you'll know, he might moan, or even mumble," he warned, taking two steps sideways to have a look from another angle. "Had a patient once who sang through his surgery. Ketamine can do some strange things sometimes."

"But they don't feel the surgery, or remember it, do they?"

"My opera singer claimed he didn't remember a thing. But I've got to tell you, I still cringe every time I hear something from the *Barber of Seville*." He glanced over at Lorna. "You OK?"

She nodded. "Just anxious to get this over with."

"Then let's do it. Get the Ketamine in him and we'll be out of here in thirty minutes."

"That fast?"

"It's a simple procedure. He'll do better once we can get him settled into a bed to rest."

"Do you do this a lot?" she asked, as she drew up the drug and injected it into the IV port.

"Amputations…no. Field surgeries, more than I want to think about. Normally we prefer to transport our criticals to an established hospital, but sometimes we don't have a choice. It's do the emergency procedure out here or nothing."

"You know I never did like surgery," she warned.

"And I never liked internal medicine."

She caught his quick glance at her over the top of his mask. Was he smiling? Had his eyes actually crinkled into a little smile?

They'd had this debate so many times over the years…surgery versus medicine. It was always a point of rivalry between the medical services, and one in which they'd indulged a time or two. To operate, or to cure by other means. The surgeons always wanted to operate first, the internal medicine doctors always chose other means first. She'd never won the debate with Gideon. But he'd never won the debate with her. "Some things never change," she said, feeling oddly nostalgic over something that shouldn't have caused even the tiniest stir in her.

"Apparently." He arched his eyebrows, and this time there was definitely a grin hiding under his mask.

As the drug seeped through the patient's system, a somber stillness dropped down over the tiny, secluded operating theater while Gideon cleansed the wound. When he was satisfied, he picked up a scalpel and took several slashes at some leg muscle while Lorna used several pads of sterile gauze to absorb the blood oozing from the wound.

She could hear Gideon's breathing through his mask…it was edgy, intense. That, in contrast to their patient, who was actually snoring quietly, like this was a pleasant midday nap for him. Gideon's eyes were narrowed in concentration, too. She remembered that look, and had always teased him it would give him early wrinkles. Which it had. The one that had pressed so deeply between his dark brown eyes was permanent now, as were the ones at the corners of his eyes. Wrinkles well earned, she guessed. And, admittedly, a little bit handsome on him. They etched character into an almost too-perfect face.

"Hemostat," he said, as he reached up to wipe the sweat from his face with his sleeve. "Two of them, actually." Briefly, he glanced over at her. "I need to fashion the muscle so that it tucks under the skin flap and covers the bone after the leg is removed."

She nodded. She knew the procedure, at least knew it from the textbooks. She'd just never wanted to be part of it, which was why she'd stayed away from surgery in every form. She did admire the surgeons, though, but she also had a particular weakness for what they did. And even now she could feel a bit of nausea welling up in her…nausea from the smell of the blood, and from thinking about the sound of the bone saw Gideon was about to use on the poor man.

"You doing OK?" he asked her once the procedure was under way. With his left hand Gideon gripped the protruding tibia with an instrument resembling large pliers, and with his right he lifted up his bone saw.

"Good enough."

He chuckled. "You used to get squeamish just reading about surgical procedures."

"You remembered that?"

"What I remember is watching you read through something particularly grisly, the way you'd turn up your nose, squint your eyes, grimace."

"Sympathetic reaction. Sometimes I could almost feel the incision." She shuddered. "Surgery wasn't my strength in medicine, and I don't deny it." Yet here she was doing the thing she dreaded most.

"You'll make it through," he said, his voice almost gentle. "Just concentrate on what you're doing and not on what I'm doing, and you'll be fine." As Gideon proceeded through the amputation, the patient began to moan and buck against his restraints.

"Could you hold him still?" he asked Lorna. "Just throw some body weight on him. Oh, and while you've got him down, take his vital signs, see how his blood-pressure is holding out. Then I'll need more gauze, and some suture."

"Anything else you'd like me to do in my spare time?" she muttered as she positioned herself to keep their patient from squirming while at the same time opening the IV drip.

As the saw made it through the last of the bone, Gideon

glanced across the operating table at Lorna. "You're the one who volunteered to do this."

"When I thought you might actually have a qualified surgical team."

"You are the qualified team, Lorna. That's the way it is out here. You step in to volunteer and you step in all the way. You don't get to pick and choose what you want to do. And I'm not trying to be cruel about this. Just honest."

Pumping up the blood-pressure cuff, she shook her head. "I didn't step in to volunteer, Gideon. I was just helping." Then she deflated the bulb and listened for the reading.

"And you think there's a difference? This isn't your pretty little world of primping for the camera and telling your audience to take vitamins. This is the real medical deal out here. What doctors and nurses and medics do who don't have to fix their hair and apply their make-up before they go to work. You step up and this is what you get."

Lorna glared at him. "You really do have a low opinion of what I do, don't you? Over the years, I thought that might have changed."

"You're a brilliant diagnostician. Always were. I never had a low opinion of that."

"But then I went and changed things. I did something I wanted to do, and you hated that."

"Didn't hate it," he mumbled.

"Didn't respect it, though. Still don't."

She waited for a response, a back down, a denial. But none came, which told her everything. She'd lost his respect the first time she'd stepped in front of the camera. All these years later, she still didn't have it.

"Suture," he said. And that was it.

Lorna found the package of suture on the surgical tray and opened it, then handed it across. Gideon worked silently for another few minutes, after which he straightened up and backed away from the table. "Bandage him up, basic amputation technique, and I'll find a couple of volunteers to take him to a bed."

Basic amputation technique? Easy for him to say! It had been years… "You can't just leave me here, Gideon! Not while he's—"

Gideon snapped off his gloves and pulled down his mask. "It'll make a nice sidebar for your story, how you jumped right in to save a life. It's not quite as glamorous as smiling for the camera, but your listeners should be impressed." Without another word he strode through the curtain, leaving her there with an unconscious patient so fresh from surgery that, technically, the surgery wasn't even over with.

"Yes, Gideon," she whispered, as she picked up the roll of gauze. "That's what you did best. You always walked away."

"What the hell do you think you're doing?" Jim Frayne yelled from the tent opening.

"Being a doctor," Lorna yelled back. Six straight hours of back and forth, from one incoming patient to another, and she'd barely had time to breathe. Six straight hours of being a doctor and of looking over her shoulder to see if Gideon was coming back. But he hadn't. Not even to check on his surgical patient. This had become her hospital tent to supervise, not by directive so much as simply stepping in and doing the work, and with the help of three local volunteers who didn't understand a word of English, the nurse called Gwen, and Brian Fontaine, a paramedic who was running back and forth between the two hospital tents, she was now caring for twenty-five casualties.

"You're not supposed to—" Frayne started.

Lorna looked over at the man. "Tell that to all these people," she snapped, frantically brushing her golden blond hair from her eyes with the back of her hand. "They're understaffed, and I can't just sit around and watch and take notes for the story when so many people need help."

"OK, OK. Be a doctor, if that's what you want to do. But just let me film it."

Certainly, that's what they were there to do. Right now, though, it seemed like such a violation. These people were injured, they'd lost homes and loved ones, and allowing her little world of media medicine into their suffering was vulgar.

"Not now," she said, kneeling down to check the pulse of one of her patients bedded on the floor. "Maybe later, when we're not so—"

"It's your job, Lorna. Not this. You didn't come here to hold hands, and I didn't come here to sit on my ass and wait for you to get off yours."

Jim Frayne was a big, burly man. Shaved head, bulging muscles, he was the best cameraman in the business, and totally devoted to his work. He was right about this…her job was to find the story, not treat the patients. Except the story would keep and her patients wouldn't. "Fine. Then take some long shots of me," she finally conceded. "No close ups of anyone *but* me. Do you understand? I don't want these people disturbed."

He shrugged. "Not much of a story from a distance. But if that's the way you want it…" He hiked his camera up and zoomed in on Lorna's face. "Smile for your audience, Doc," he said.

Instead of smiling, she spun around to have a look at the patient behind her…a young boy separated from his family. He was more frightened than injured, but there was no place else for him right now. The village streets were still clogged with people hoping to find surviving family members and good-hearted volunteers bringing in food and fresh water. Among them, Cristovão, as he called himself, would get lost. So for now he had a bed. And tomorrow… She didn't want to think about that. "I wish you could understand me," she said, as she checked the bump on his head. It wasn't a nasty gash, but she knew his head had to be aching something terrible.

"They understand in actions and smiles," Gideon said, finally coming back in to check on his surgical patient.

Lorna looked up at him. "He's got to be scared to death."

"I think most of the people who survive something like this are." He grabbed a blood-pressure cuff and took the man's reading, then listened to his chest. After, he pulled back the sheet and looked at the wrapped leg. "Any bleeding?" he asked.

"Not excessive. Vitals have been stable, blood-pressure normalizing. He's been asleep…"

Gideon nodded. "I'd have been back sooner, but I was up on the south face, helping pull a family of five out of the…"

Lorna held up her hand to stop him. "You don't have to explain it to me," she said. "I knew you'd get back when you could."

"About earlier, some of the things I said…"

She shook her head. "Don't, Gideon. It was bad enough when we went through it all before. Let's just leave it alone here. OK? So, those five people you helped pull out?"

He frowned. "Fine. Not injured other than scratches and scrapes. The house above them came right down on theirs, but they were lucky."

"Why do they live like that, all stacked up?"

"Free land essentially, and you can't blame them. People all over the world do it—build in places that go against nature. But comes the rain and they wash out. Look at what happens in California during rainy season. Huge mansions sliding right off the mountain face, only the houses aren't stacked up one on top of another like they are here. The lure of the land prevails, though, and people don't think about the consequences. And here, in this area, which is overpopulated to begin with, where no one rightfully claims the land and it's basically there for the taking, they take it." He held his hand out to help her up. "You need to take a break."

"I'm fine," she said stiffly.

"We take breaks," he said. "Two hours every six, not negotiable unless the boss says otherwise, or unless you're out on an active rescue."

"Except you're not my boss." She studied his hand for a moment, then rose without taking it. "You don't get your way with me, Gideon. Not anymore." Admittedly, she was tired to the bone from the most frantic medical pace she'd ever experienced in her life, which made two hours off sound like a mighty tempting offer. Had anyone other than Gideon suggested it, she would have gladly given in and been half asleep by now. But because this was Gideon…"I'm perfectly capable of another few hours of work, in spite of what you think of me as the media doctor."

"What I think of the doctor who makes call-in diagnoses on national television doesn't matter here, but what I think of a field doctor who's just worked six hours for my response team does. And what I think is that you're inexperienced at this, therefore you're relieved of duty. Two hours off. If you're still here after that, you're welcome to come back and work for another six."

"What do you mean, if I'm still here?"

"Haven't you got your story yet? You've seen the suffering. Your man has filmed his share of it. So now you can go back to New York and act like an expert on what we do here. Isn't that the purpose of this trip? To put yourself in the middle of a disaster to boost your television ratings and let your audience know you're still a real doctor?

"How dare you?" she snarled.

"I dare any damned thing I please, Lorna. If you stay, get used to it because there's more where that came from." He turned to walk away, then paused. "The row of tents out behind the food tent…sleep in any of them that has room. We don't pick bedmates, and we don't get private quarters. There's a wooden floor down and some bedding. I'd suggest you use it. If you choose not to, do whatever you want. Just don't do it anywhere near my base camp."

Stunned, Lorna watched Gideon march though the door and disappear into the darkness outside. When had he turned so hard? Sure, there had been problems when they'd divorced…problems, bitter feelings, harsh words. But never, ever had he acted this way. Was she bringing out the worst in him, or was he always like this when he was out on a rescue? One thing was for sure—she certainly didn't know the man who'd once been her husband. Not when they'd been married. Not now.

"He means what he says," Priscilla Getty, Jason's wife, called to Lorna on her way inside to relieve her for the next two hours. "Gideon's a stickler for procedure. He's fair, but he keeps order, which makes him just about the best in the world at what he does." A soft smile brushed over her lips. "Like my Jason."

Lorna took an immediate liking to Priscilla. She was a pretty woman. Blond like her husband, and tall, she was a good match for him physically. And the look in her eyes as she spoke of him…Lorna almost envied that. She might have had that same look for a time when she'd been with Gideon, but honestly, she couldn't remember it if she had. "He gets away with acting like that even though everyone here is a volunteer? I'd think he'd treat people better."

"Actually, he treats people quite well. I think you were just on the receiving end of a long, bad day. And Gideon really doesn't like public attention, so you're getting that fallout, too." She poured a cup of water from the cooler sitting in the middle aisle, then took it over to a young woman bedded on the floor. Bending down, Priscilla straightened her blankets then handed her the cup. "I think because everyone here is a volunteer, it's easy to overwork yourself when there's so much to do," she continued. "You come here because you want to help, but if you don't take care of yourself, you're no good to anyone. So Gideon sees to it that we take care of ourselves, even if he seems a little testy doing it. But he does care." After the woman had taken her water, she patted Priscilla's hand, said something Lorna didn't understand but took to be a thank-you, and shut her eyes to sleep.

"You'll like him when you get to know him better," Priscilla said, moving on to the next patient in the row. "Let me rephrase that a bit…when Gideon lets you get to know him. That's the other thing about him…most of the time he keeps people at an arm's length."

Lorna poured a cup of water and handed it to Priscilla, who bent down to tuck in the next patient and give him a drink. "How long have you and Jason been doing this?" she asked.

"Almost since the day we were married. Jason's an ear, nose and throat specialist. Nice practice, but rather boring, I think, and he needed a higher calling. Being the newlywed that I was, I didn't want to be separated from him so I tagged along when he joined First Responders. That's where we met Gideon. We kept bumping into him on rescues. Then Gideon took over Global Response and asked Jason to come over as his partner." She shrugged. "It's what I do. I don't have a lot to contribute medically except some basic care, but I like making a difference where I can, and I'm pretty good at the rescue end of it."

"And your marriage survives," Lorna commented. That, in itself, was a miracle.

"It survives, and even thrives." She gave Lorna a cheery smile. "Go take a nap. You really do need it."

Lorna handed her stethoscope over to Priscilla. "Maybe you're right. Maybe I do need it."

And who knew? Two hours without thinking of Gideon might be just what the doctor ordered, since all she'd been doing for the past six hours had been thinking about him.

CHAPTER THREE

THE volunteers' tent row consisted of several rounded domes sitting up off the soggy ground on wooden planks. Each nylon tent would hold two people, three if you didn't mind sleeping on top of each other, literally, and as Lorna soon discovered, the tents that were zipped up all the way were occupied. After checking the first two, she found the third one unzipped, so she peeked inside to make sure she wasn't intruding, then tossed in her backpack and crawled straight into the bedding on the left side. It was a very cozy arrangement with little room to separate her from whoever would be sleeping in there with her. It was kind of a throwback to those early days in the hospital on-call room, where, after a very long shift on duty, any open bed was welcome, and it didn't matter who slept next to you so long as they didn't snore too loudly, sleepwalk or, worst of all, talk. And actually, during her medical residency, when she'd been required to work long, consecutive shifts without leaving the hospital, and sleep had been a luxury that had been taken wherever and whenever she could get it, snoring, walking and talking aside, by the time she'd usually bunked down in an on-call room, she had been so tired that a band of marching bagpipers coming through wouldn't have disturbed her.

Tonight, after she'd finally admitted it to herself that she was even more tired than she could remember, that heap of bedding on top of a stopgap wooden floor felt almost as good as goose-down. It didn't take Lorna any time at all to pull off her rain-soaked clothes, slip into a pair of dry ones from her pack, and snuggle down into the blankets. Heaven on a wooden floor.

Was Frayne bedding down for the night, too? She hadn't thought about him for a while, she'd been so busy, but she wasn't awfully worried about him. As much as they worked together, they worked even more than that apart, and she was sure that he was fending for himself quite nicely. Just the way Gideon was fending for himself. It was a hard life that Gideon had chosen, she was just now coming to discover, but this was everything he'd ever wanted. *Everything he'd wanted, more than he'd wanted her.* She was sure he was happy this way, doing the thing he loved most in the world, which was good because she didn't, in the least, begrudge him his happiness. As miserable as they'd been at the end of their marriage, she'd never wished him anything bad. Actually, she was glad he had this. He was a good man who deserved his happiness.

It was funny how, after so much time, the marriage wounds she'd thought long since healed actually ached a bit. "Proximity," she mumbled into her pillow, as she turned over on her side, her back to the center of the tent, and pulled herself into a ball. An unex-pected proximity to Gideon was all it could be. Old pains resurfac-ing, possibly a few unresolved feelings nagging. It was natural, she decided. After all, they had planned a life and made a baby together. She was entitled to some leftover emotions, even after all this time.

Lorna's eyes weren't even closed when someone else crawled into the tent. For a moment, she thought about making pleasan-tries since they would be sleeping together these next two hours, but she decided to forgo it since the other person didn't so much as mumble a hello to her. Maybe that was the protocol with Gideon's people. Crawl in, sleep, crawl back out. Most likely, her roomie was as bone tired as she was…someone more interested in sleep than chat. Did she know that feeling!

Tugging her blanket up to her chin, Lorna shut her eyes and let out a little sigh.

"You always did that," her companion said. "Let out that sigh right when you were on the verge of going to sleep."

Her eyes snapped right back open. "What did you do? Watch which tent I chose then follow me in?" He nudged at her back, and she scooted closer to the tent side. "And don't touch me, Gideon. Sleeping with me back then doesn't give you the right to do so much as breathe on me now!"

"Believe me, if I'd known you were in here, I'd have slept in the rain if there weren't any other open beds."

"Weren't you supposed to be out on rescue or something?"

"Dani took watch. Dag, her dog, was up for it. Max was a little tired, and the dogs get the same consideration as the people. When it's time to rest, they rest."

He nudged at her back again, this time a little harder, and she could feel him settle in, almost back to back with her. "Come on, Gideon. Just stay on your side of the tent. OK?" The argument was futile. Most of them with Gideon had been because no one won. Normally, they'd fight until they were tired of it, then they'd give in and make up by…No! She wasn't going to dwell on *that!* Sometimes the making up seemed the point of the argument.

"Hey, if you don't like the arrangement, go find yourself another spot,"

"I was here first."

"I suppose this is the place where I could raise the argument that I own the tent, but I won't because all I want to do is grab a couple hours' sleep. So, at the risk of starting an argument that we already know we'd be brilliant at dragging out for the whole two hours, all I have to say is if you don't want to utilize your two hours off, that's up to you. But, please, allow me mine."

As he said the words, he pushed himself even more into her back…close enough that she could feel the heat of him through her blanket. Then…Dear God! What was that sliding across the back of her neck? "Gideon," she snarled, rolling over into a large…very large…dog. "Max?" she asked, pushing away from him just as his tongue caught her across the face.

Hearing his name, Max took that as an open invitation to join her, and rolled over, laying his head across her chest. "Would you get him off me?" she sputtered, not sure how the dog would respond if she tried forcing him.

"He doesn't take to very many people that way. You should consider yourself fortunate," Gideon replied, laughing.

"Just get him off me," she muttered, still too wary to move. "I'll go sleep somewhere else and you two can have the whole tent to yourselves if you'll just get him off me!"

"He's very stubborn. Don't know if he'll obey me."

"Do it, Gideon! Just get the dog!"

"But I thought you liked dogs. Didn't we even talk about getting a puppy once?"

"A puppy weighs a hundred pounds less," she said, starting to ease herself away from the dog. "And doesn't smell like…"

"A wet dog?" Gideon volunteered, still laughing.

"OK, so the dog comes first. I get it. But he's your dog, let him sleep on top of you."

"Maybe we should have had a dog. Might have mellowed you a little."

Might have kept her company, too. "I would have loved a dog, except I didn't have time to train one, and you were never there…" Drawing in a deep breath, Lorna finally pulled herself out from underneath Max's enormous head, gave him a quick scratch behind the ears to show him there were no hard feelings intended, grabbed her pack and started crawling for the door.

"No other beds available this shift," Gideon said.

"Then I'll sleep outside in the rain." Unzipping the door, she took one look outside and saw that the ground directly in front of the tent had turned into a rivulet. Damn, she hated rain. More than that, she hated this rain.

"Just zip the door," Gideon said. "I promise I won't let Max cuddle in with you again." He snapped his fingers, and Max instantly stood, took two steps and plopped down next to Gideon. "Now, go to sleep."

"Who? Me, or your dog?" Lorna gave in and crawled back over to her bedding, pulled up the blanket, turned her back on Gideon and Max, then let out a weary little sigh.

"You always did that," Gideon said. Then the tent went still.

But in the dark, huddled into a ball on her side of the tent, with the rain beating down on the outside and man and beast snoring lightly at her back, Lorna's head was filled with too many memories to drop right off to sleep.

Her eyes blinked open. Not again! She couldn't have been dozing more than ten minutes, finally, and now that dog was trying to lick her face again. Debating her options, Lorna reached up to wipe the dog slobber away, deciding that this time she'd camp out anywhere but here. Even under the bench in the food tent would be better than this. "I've had enough," she said wearily, as she rolled over. Just as she did, a splash of water hit her neck and rolled down the side of it.

Immediately, Lorna glanced up, but it was too dark in the tent to see anything. So she rose up on her knees, stretching out her arm to the top of the tent. Sure enough, her fingers felt the perceptible dampness, and broke up the next drop getting ready to burst loose from the fabric and hit her. Naturally, she was the lucky one with the bed under the leak.

She thought about waking Gideon up, but in all fairness, there was nothing he could do except heckle her or tell her to go away.

So why bother? Besides, there was surely enough room in here to sleep in another spot, or at an angle where the water would miss her. So Lorna scooted all the way over to the side of the tent and turned on her side. Unfortunately, the next drop skimmed down the back of her neck. And the next hit the top of her head as she tried to move closer to the door. Then to the center next to Max, who responded with a doggy kiss to her cheek.

"You're wasting my two hours," Gideon muttered. "There are a lot of reasons to waste my sleep time but, believe me, what you're doing isn't one of them."

"And your stupid tent is wasting mine."

"I take it you found the leak."

"More like the leak found me." She fumbled with the bedding, pulling it out of the way of the infernal drip, hoping to keep it dry, if not for her then for the next unsuspecting victim forced to sleep in that spot.

"Here," Gideon said, rolling over and handing her a pot. "We keep these in all the tents. One of the things we plan on doing if your documentary succeeds in raising us some funds is buying a new round of tents. Until then, stick a pot under it."

As she tried to figure out where best to put it, and various parts of Gideon's anatomy weren't out of the question, Gideon reared up, pulled her bedding away from her, then lay right back down. "Just put it under the drip then, if it's your intention to salvage what's left of your two hours, come over on my side. There's room between Max and me. And for God's sake, don't provoke him. He needs his sleep, too."

"Me provoke him?" Never had trying to catch a little sleep been so difficult. But Lorna was so tired she was well past the point of argument, and right now she would have slept with a dozen snoring dogs if that's what it would have taken. Actually, a dozen snoring dogs would have been preferable to Gideon. But Gideon's invitation was all she had, and it really wasn't such a big deal. After all, they'd done it before. And at the end of their marriage that's all they'd done in their bed. So she'd just pretend this was the end of their marriage again, and crawl in next to him with the absolute certainty that sleep would be the only outcome. Sleep, or another inadvertent shower.

Taking Gideon up on his invitation, Lorna shoved the small aluminum pot under the drip, crawled past Max, who hadn't budged, and wedged herself in between man and beast. Then she grabbed up her blanket and pillow, stuffed the pillow under her head, wrapped the blanket around her, and shut her eyes.

And listened to the still, perfect rhythm of Gideon's breathing.

He wasn't asleep. It was so easy to tell with him because when he slept his breaths were long and deep. These were shallow, almost staccato in their precision. They matched exactly the ping of the drops hitting the pot. Was this closeness making him nervous? Was he afraid she'd want to talk about something deep and personal, like what a failure he'd been in their marriage?

A slight smile touched Lorna's lips as she turned over on her side and spooned him...better spooning Gideon than Max. In that instant when her body slid into his, she heard a slight groan from him. "You always did that," she said. "Let out that groan when you were on the verge of something other than sleep."

"Sweet dreams, Lorna," he said, his voice rough. "And for what it's worth, you did a good job in surgery. Thank you for pitching in to help us."

For what it was worth? It was worth a lot. Contented, Lorna let out a sigh as she closed her eyes.

"You always did that," he said.

Then neither of them spoke.

"Sleep well?" Frayne asked.

In the food tent, sitting on a wooden bench with a wooden crate serving as her table, Lorna looked at him through barely opened eyes as she grasped her mugful of coffee like it was the very essence of her life. Her hair wasn't combed, her clothes were wrinkled, her eyes puffy. All this after only two hours of fitful sleep. What she wouldn't have given for a nice hot bath right about then. Or a good cup of coffee instead of this muddy brew they called coffee. After all, this was Brazil. Weren't the coffee beans here among the best in the world? She took another sip of the pitch-black, molasses-thick liquid and smacked her lips after the bitter taste. Apparently, it didn't matter how good the beans were when the coffee was made like this. "Let's just say that I had some intermittent sleep, and leave it at that. Did you bed down?"

"Not yet. Did some night-time filming, and I think I'll keep on going for another couple of hours before I crash."

"Tent on the end has a leak, and it smells like a wet dog," she muttered.

"Sounds like you had a jolly time of it."

"Jolly," she muttered, then took another sip of coffee, turning up her nose at it as she forced herself to swallow. "Anything come in while I was down?"

"A few patients that I saw. Don't think they were serious, but the crew here is keeping me away from the medical tents. There's a general opinion about that we're intrusive. The one called Gideon is downright hostile about the camera. He threatened to smash it if he caught me filming around him again." He snorted. "Like he could!"

Leave it to Gideon to make friends everywhere he went. Actually, she didn't blame him so much for the attitude. Their job here *was* to be intrusive. "How many casualties?" she asked.

"Forty-seven injured, nine of them critical. And hundreds missing. No accurate count on that yet, since the people are still moving around, finding shelter in the churches in town, going to friends and family."

Hundreds missing. However it turned out, and wherever they

were, the thought of that caused her to shiver. The first of this mud slide had happened nearly forty-eight hours ago, and the prospects for those not yet rescued who might have suffered injury…she didn't even want to think about it. "Maybe most of them made it up to the town," she said, trying to sound optimistic, although feeling anything but.

"Or didn't," Frayne responded rather flatly.

"So you don't believe in being an optimist?"

He shrugged. "I take pictures. My world revolves around what I see, and I've seen some awful things in my time. I expect I was an optimist when I started out. Most of us in the media are. But that was a damn long time ago, and I've seen too much." Frayne stood. "Come daylight, I want to get some footage of you doing whatever it is you're going to be doing. I've got plenty of background material, but I don't have you, and if we're going to get out of here by afternoon, we don't have a lot of time to waste. So what you might want to do is think about putting some script together and concentrating on exactly where you want me to film you. I'm thinking a shot among some of the ruined houses would be good. Maybe standing on the roof of one of the flattened ones. That'll set up a good visual, I think."

"We're leaving in the afternoon?" She knew it was to be a fast trip, but nobody had told her how fast. She was only the talent, the one before the camera. Frayne was the producer, the one who was actually in charge of the shoot.

Frayne blinked his surprise. "You didn't think we'd come down here for the duration, did you? They want this on air this weekend, which doesn't give us much time."

Actually, she didn't know what she'd thought. But apparently it didn't matter. In another sixteen or so hours she'd be on her way back to New York, to her real life. That was probably a good thing, but the curious part was she felt a little uncomfortable about it, like she was letting the people here down—volunteers and medical staff alike. None were her responsibility, of course. And Gideon hadn't even wanted her there to begin with. So hopping on the transport that would take her back to the helicopter that would take her to the airplane that would take her to New York was probably the smartest thing to do. Still, she felt uncomfortable, and maybe even a bit disappointed. "Give me some warning so I can make myself presentable for the camera," she said, raising the coffee to her lips, then changing her mind and setting it down on the wooden crate. "I'll be in one of the hospital tents."

Priscilla was still there, watching over the patients, as Lorna walked through the door. "Two hours goes by pretty fast," Priscilla said. "Every twenty-four hours, we sleep for four, which is a little better." She was sitting on the floor, holding a small child in her arms, the way only a mother could do. The child was sound asleep, with the look of an angel on her face—a look that belied trouble, pain, suffering. "We haven't found her family yet. One of the volunteers found her a while ago, and we'll keep her for a while before we send her on to the authorities. People know to come here to look," she said, brushing a strand of black hair back from the child's face.

"There's nothing wrong with her?" Lorna asked.

"Jason took a look, and she's fine." She smiled sadly. "Fine, except that she's not with her mother."

"Does she have a name?" Lorna scooped the child from Priscilla's arms, and the transfer didn't even cause the child to stir. Poor thing had to be exhausted, she thought.

"I've been calling her Estella. She's too young to correct me." Priscilla stood, gave Estella a kiss on the cheek, then headed for the door. "I'm going to catch a couple of hours' sleep, then we're taking the dogs out come first light." She glanced up at the nighttime sky, as if she could see the stormclouds up there. "All this rain…I don't even want to think what we'll find in the morning."

"Do you miss your children?" Lorna asked.

"All the time. It's not easy, leaving them."

"But yet you do."

"They're well cared for, and Jason and I don't always go out on the same rescues. I like to think that someday, when they're old enough to understand why we leave them from time to time, they'll be proud of what their parents do." She gave a faint smile, then looked at Lorna. "You don't have any children, do you?"

Lorna shook her head as she cradled Estella. "Some people just aren't meant for it."

"No one in your life to change your mind about that?"

"I have my work." Lorna watched Priscilla until she disappeared into the night, continuing to cradle the child, wishing she had a stuffed bear for Estella to cuddle. Maybe when Estella's mother came for her, she'd bring one. *If her mother came for her*.

Gideon stopped just outside the opening to the tent and looked in rather than entering. It was a sight he hadn't expected, and one that shouldn't have bothered him. But seeing Lorna sitting there, cradling and rocking a baby, knocked the breath out of him. She would have been a beautiful mother. Even now, with someone else's child, she fairly glowed. And the expression on her face as she talked to the child—or was she singing a lullaby?—was as close to perfect contentment as he'd ever seen.

He tried not to think about it too often, about losing their child. Sometimes, though, in the empty moments, he still fantasized what it would have been like, being a father. At times he pictured himself as a father to a little boy, playing ball and all the games little boys liked to play. Often, that fantasy was so real that when he opened his eyes to find it was only a daydream he became physically ill. Then there were times when he was the father of a beautiful little girl. She looked like Lorna—same smile, same wide blue eyes. Then his heart broke because that would never happen.

Did Lorna still think about it? Did her heart still break?

Gideon watched until Lorna laid the child down in a pile of soft bedding, then kiss her gently on the cheek, before he turned and walked away. He'd been angry and hurt when they'd lost the baby. He'd felt cheated. Now he just felt empty. As much as he loved Max, a dog simply didn't fill the void. And that void had become so much bigger now that Lorna was here.

Sighing, Gideon headed over to the food tent for a bitter cup of coffee, then wandered over to the supply tent to check the rescue grid and plot the next group out. As he passed by the hospital tent, he didn't look in at Lorna, didn't look in at the child she still sat with. He couldn't. Not right now. Not while the fantasy of Lorna sitting next to the bed of *their* child, singing a gentle lullaby, was ripping at his heart.

She'd seen Gideon wander by twice, pausing outside for a few minutes once, and had thought he might stop in. But he hadn't. Honestly, she wasn't even sure why that disappointed her, but it did. Right now the whole thing between them seemed almost…she grappled for the right word. Friendly? No, that wasn't it. Mellow, perhaps? That seemed good. Thinking that she and Gideon were mellow with each other felt right. Comfortable. The beginning of something different. "So you're the resident veterinarian?" Lorna asked Dani. Frayne was standing off to the side, filming, and for once Lorna had opted to go *sans* make-up. Truth was, she was too busy to worry, and tossing this little interview into the middle of her work was almost an annoyance. But Dani and the nurse named Tom had a few minutes and Frayne had nabbed them for a quick interview.

Dani beamed at the camera. "Someone has to take care of the dogs, and when we travel, depending upon who's on call, we can sometimes have up to five with us."

"But you're also a paramedic?" Lorna asked. "Medically trained outside your veterinary practice?"

"Fully trained and qualified. Having the qualifications to work on humans makes me a little more useful, I think."

Lorna turned to Tom McCain. Handsome man, tall, fair complexion, bright eyes. A real draw to the camera. "And you're a registered nurse?"

"Yes. Seven years now."

"So what first attracted you to rescue work?"

"Anything that gets me outside is good. I like the break from the normal routine, which, on my regular days, is as a critical care nurse. One day, I saw an article in a medical journal about what people are doing in the rescue field, and signed up the next day." He grinned at Dani. "Glad I did. So far, it's all good."

Lorna asked a couple more questions of Dani and Tom, then ended the interview. They were a cute couple and anyone who watched the segment would see that look in their eyes. "So tell me," she said once they were off camera, "how do you find time for a social life?"

Tom laughed. "This is it. A few minutes between rescues...You don't get much so you have to make the most of what you get." He and Dani said a quick goodbye with a very proper kiss, and Dani went off to check the dogs while Tom followed Lorna into the tent.

"And you get used to it?" Lorna asked.

"Not so much used to it as immune to it." He picked up a medication order tacked to the chart of a little old man complaining of back pain. "Makes you appreciate more what you get," he said, then dashed off to the medical supply for a dose of ibuprofen, darting past Gideon, who was bringing in an armload of bedding from Supply.

"They're lucky to still be so optimistic," Gideon said as he moved past Lorna.

"We were like that once," she said on a wistful sigh. "Remember?"

"Like that? Those two are starry-eyed. We were merely…" He handed the bedding to Gwen who whooshed by him, then bent over to Lorna and whispered, "Horny."

Her eyes widened in surprise. "Nothing wrong with that," she said, fighting back a laugh. Truth was, he was right. They had been. Chemistry and passion had prevailed at the starting gate of their relationship and the rest of it never had a chance to catch up. "Except getting married because of it."

"I seem to recall a few good moments out of bed," he countered.

"Odd," she quipped, heading across the tent to take a temperature of one of the children brought in earlier. "I don't seem to recall *any* moments out of bed. Of course, I've spent five years trying not to recall pretty much anything of our marriage." Except the part where he'd had his goals for himself, and he'd also had his goals for *her*. Goals that hadn't been hers. Somehow, that had never gone away because one thing she'd learned over the years had been that out of sight didn't necessarily mean out of mind. And as much as she wanted to lie to Gideon about it, and even to herself, he'd never really been out of her mind.

CHAPTER FOUR

"I DIDN'T expect it to be so tough," Lorna commented to Gideon, after he'd done the latest round of assessments for half the patients in the tent while she did the same for the others.

Blood-pressure, heart rate, respiration count...they'd worked well together. Hadn't said much, concentrating on their tasks, but in an odd sort of way, working alongside Gideon had been satisfying. They hadn't argued, hadn't had cross words, hadn't even tipped in the direction of antagonism. One hour of working together had been good. "Nobody does at first," Gideon whispered, so as not to rouse the sleeping patients, as he stopped behind Lorna while she helped an old man take a drink of cool water. "But you learn. First time out, you learn." She was being an awfully good sport about this, much better than he'd thought she could be. Actually, he'd underestimated her because she'd been good the whole time she'd been there. Not at all like the Lorna he'd expected—the Lorna who spent as much time preening for the camera as he did performing an appendectomy.

He thought about what he'd expected. Glitz. Primping and pampering. Admittedly, she'd never been that bad when they'd been married, but over the years, as he'd watched her on the telly, he'd indulged himself in some exaggerations about her, namely the ones where she'd betrayed herself by turning herself into a media spectacle. Of course, that was pure wounded pride talking. He knew that. As for the glitz he'd expected, well, what he'd seen so far had been grit, not glitz. Pure grit. While he wasn't ready to admit it out loud, he was gaining a new respect for Lorna, and her abilities. She was damned good. Willing, hard-working and damned good.

Funny how he'd never noticed that about her when they'd been married. If anyone had even hinted that Lorna might do well in the rescue field, he would have laughed.

And he would have been wrong.

"Do you ever get used to it?" she asked. "After all this time, does any of it ever get to you or are you pretty much impervious?"

"Get used to it? In a way, I suppose you do. But it still gets to you. Every response is different while the emotions are always the same. And I think if you ever get to the point where it doesn't get to you, it's time to quit. This is a job where you have to feel it every moment, have to have the passion to do it. When you don't feel it, the passion's gone, and let me tell you, the only thing that gets you through sometimes is the passion for the work. There's no glamour here, no recognition, no reward other than the outcome, and conditions are hard. We're sleep deprived half the time, we ache physically, we put our own lives on the line more than any of us care to think about. And without exception we make personal sacrifices in our lives to do this." He paused for a moment, thinking back to the day Lorna had miscarried. He should have been there, should have stood at her bedside holding her hand. But that simple gesture was counted among the sacrifices, and in terms of his life, it had been a huge one. And one that still caused him to ache. "So, there are a lot of things you do get used to, but so many more that you can't if you want to survive emotionally."

"And have you survived emotionally?" she asked.

"Better than most, I think. I don't have another life to return to. For me, this is it. No conflicts, no divisions, no tugging back and forth for my time. I think that makes it easier." Or emptier.

Lorna turned to face Gideon, and was immediately confronted by Max. This was the first she'd seen of him in the light, and he was nearly as big as she was. Beautiful dog. Soulful eyes. Huggable. "What is he?" she asked, bending down and taking that hug.

"A brindle mastiff," he said, smiling with pride "Picked him up from a rescue society. Somebody had abused him."

She stayed bent down, petting him. "I though you used bloodhounds when you tracked people."

"Some people do, and they're the best for pure tracking, especially if you have a scent for them to follow. But tracking isn't search and rescue, and for that we use any dog with good instincts. A search-and-rescue dog has to have a keen sense of knowing that a victim is somewhere nearby. For Max, he gets excited, has a certain impatient whine. He displays a whole set of subtle signs when he's on the hunt for a live victim…has different subtle signs when the one he's hunting isn't alive. And, yes, he does know the difference." He gave Max a pat on the head after Lorna stood and immediately Max leaned into Gideon's thigh, looking up at him in doggy adoration. "Max is as good as they get."

"And you take him everywhere?"

"As long as it's not a danger to him, yes. Look, I'm going out on night patrol. Going to walk the perimeters of the south section and see what I can find. We don't do a full search at night because it's too dangerous, but sometimes you can pick up on something, especially when it's quiet, like it is now." A playful smile crossed his face. "Not taking Max. Want to come in his place?"

She bit back her own smile. "So you protect your dog, but when it comes to your ex-wife…"

"When it comes to my ex-wife I'd say she's an admirable stand-in," he teased.

"I'm not sure if I should take that as a compliment."

"Take it as an invitation to see, firsthand, what we do. I'd like to show you." He meant it. He did want to show Lorna some of the operation. He was proud of his team and for some strange reason he wanted to share that with her...share it with Lorna the doctor and the ex-wife, not the television reporter.

"If I go with you, who's going to watch the patients here?"

"Dani's still up. And Tom's available. I'm sure they won't object to some time together."

"I thought you didn't want me getting in your way."

He took Max by the leash, signaled him to stand, and headed to the door of the tent. "You won't, if you do what I tell you."

"And walk two paces behind you, like that good subservient ex-wife that I am?"

"And walk ten paces to the side of me to look for something I might have missed."

"Nobody out here knows you were married, do they?" she asked.

"No reason they should." Especially since, most of the time, he tried not to think about it. "Are you coming?"

That was an almost amiable interchange, she thought as she slogged through the mud several paces abreast of Gideon. Max was crated for now. Gideon said they didn't take the dogs out in the dark unless absolutely necessary because it was too risky. Gideon would go out, but he kept his dog safe. Somehow, that didn't surprise her. He took care of the people here. Not just the patients, but the volunteers. He was like...a protective father. A lump formed in her throat, thinking about it. He was the way with them that he would have been with their child.

It was odd, how he cared so passionately. Odd, the way she'd never seen that in him when they'd been together—the year before their marriage, and the two years during it. She thought back to the last few weeks before they'd separated, while they'd still been hanging on, even though they'd both known there had been no point. Fighting over nothing, fighting over everything...

In all honesty, they'd had more interaction then than they'd had during the times when they'd been happy together.

It was so strange, she thought, the way they'd gone up and down. Some of the swings she could account for—the miscarriage, the change of her career direction. Gideon hadn't been happy about the change. As for the miscarriage…it hadn't caused the breakup of their marriage, but it had become the convenient excuse. The last in a long line of marital disappointments. And honestly, by that time, it had already been inevitable. A baby might have breathed new life into their relationship, but for how long?

"So when you and Max go out together, who leads? she asked.

"He does. But not on a leash. They leash the tracking dogs, but he's not tracking. He's searching. So he's allowed a wide berth within reason, under my command, of course. He leads, I follow him."

"But he'll come back if you call him?"

"He's well trained, and obedient." He chuckled. "And he knows who feeds him."

"All the qualities of the wife you always wanted and never had," she quipped, and he smiled. "Anyway, tell me what I'm supposed to do out in the field."

"Walk, and observe. Since it's still dark, listen. That's the most important sense."

"Sounds easy enough."

"Never easy, Lorna. Trust me, what we do here is never easy."

Like what she did on her job was easy? She wanted to ask him if that's what he thought, but this wasn't the time. People here needed help, and opening old wounds simply got in the way. They'd had their arguments and it was in the past, buried the way so much of this little area was buried. Only here there was still some hope left for the rescue. With their marriage, the mud was far too deep to dig it out. As if she would do that, if she could.

* * *

They walked in silence for better than an hour. Slowly, methodically, they made their way over the soupy terrain, only to go back and retrace their steps two, sometimes three times before they moved on to the next area. Through it all, the only sound nearby was that of their shoes squishing about in the mud. It was a constant rhythm, with Gideon making considerably more noise than she was. Each step was small, calculated. Each step was painfully slow, as if dreading what the next step would bring.

They hadn't gone off far from the encampment, really. The light of it trailed along at their backs, the sounds of the suffering there blown off in the opposite direction by the wind. Occasionally the wail of someone suffering, or frightened, pricked through the stillness. But mostly there was silence, except for the noises they made trudging in the mud.

Suddenly, Gideon stopped. Reacting to his abrupt movement, Lorna stopped instantly and the gooseflesh rose immediately on her arms, causing the slight brush of her skin against the fabric of her sleeves to heighten in her nervousness. "What?" she whispered.

"Did you hear it?" he asked.

She listened, didn't hear a thing. Even so, she sucked in her breath and held it for fear that even the tiniest bit of sound would cover up what he was listening to.

"Above us," Gideon said, taking hold of Lorna's hand and pulling her toward him. "Somewhere up on the ridge, not too far up there."

She squeezed his hand hard in the nervous anticipation that they were about to make a rescue. "Was it a person?" It could have been the shifting of a collapsed structure. Or someone savaging the ruins for a souvenir or a treasured memory from their wreckage. Or it could have been Gideon's imagination, except she didn't believe that at all. He was too good to make that kind of a mistake.

"Female," he said.

Lorna sucked in another deep breath, held it, shut her eyes and listened again. That's when she heard it, just the barest scrap of a whimper—one so imperceptibly faint she might have walked on by and thought it nothing. Except it wasn't nothing. Gideon knew that, too, judging from the way his spine went stiff. "I can't tell where it's coming from," Lorna started, still not sure what to make of it.

"Shh," he warned, silencing her. He let go of her hand and turned in a circle, stopping with every step to listen until he faced in a direction from which he didn't move. "This way," he said, pointing his torch at Lorna and motioning her over, then pointing it at a spot in the rubble. "It's coming from there."

Instinctively, Lorna looked up, trying to remember what she'd seen there earlier when it had been light, since all she saw right now was black. Nothing came to mind other than mud, though. Mud and several collapsed structures. "Gideon, how do we get her out? We can't just walk up there. We could cause something to break loose, knock something down on where she is…" The actual rescue had never occurred to her. The medical aftermath was all she'd ever considered. But now here she was, faced with a woman who might need medical care but who couldn't even get out of wherever she was. And who could die if her rescuers made the wrong move.

A cold chill twined up her spine. "What do we do?"

"Well, for starters, use that gift of chatter," he said. Then he clicked on his two-way radio. "South face, half a kilometer from base. We need digging tools, light, and a stretcher. And bring Max up. We have a survivor somewhere around here!"

"You want me to chatter with her?" Lorna asked after his radio was tucked away.

"Something like that. Do it loud so she can hear you wherever she is. Another voice encourages a response, which will help us locate her. Also, something else we've learned is that a person is a lot more calm if someone merely talks to them. It's knowing that they're not alone…so let her know she's not alone any longer. Reassure her that we will get her out."

"And if she doesn't understand me?"

He gave her an affectionate squeeze to the shoulder. "Trust me, she might not understand the words, but she'll understand. Kindness is a universal language, Lorn, and you're a kind person. She'll understand that, if nothing else."

Behind them, Lorna could hear the sloppy pounding of numerous feet in the mud. They were so fast to respond. Gideon called, and they were on their way in less than a minute. She couldn't help be impressed, and overwhelmed. They were coming prepared to do their part of the rescue, but she had her very own part in it. Talk. It's what she did for a living, but suddenly it had never seemed so important. "We're coming for you! Don't give up, it won't be much longer," she called out as Gideon walked a cautious path up the embankment, trying to discover where the woman was.

"Louder," he shouted over the growing noise of the crowd gathering there. "She's not answering."

Panic gripped her. To have come so close then to have the woman die…No! She wasn't going to think like that. "It's only going to take another few minutes, then we'll have you out of there," she said, louder this time. "I know you're frightened. I would be, too. But Gideon is on his way. He'll find you, then we'll take you back to camp and take good care of you. Although I hope you don't like coffee because what they make there is terrible. Worst I've ever had."

Up ahead, Gideon stopped for a moment. "Quiet," he said, and Lorna assumed he was listening for another sound from the woman.

She was quiet for several seconds before she heard Gideon snarl, "Damn it!" Meaning no sign of the woman yet.

"OK, talk again," he called to her.

Which she did. "But if you like coffee, I promise I'll make a fresh pot of it for you…the right way. And the food is delicious. I can vouch for that. As soon as we get you back, we'll get you looked at, get you into a nice, warm shower, then…"

"Quiet," Gideon cautioned again, and Lorna immediately went still. She waited, her nerves so brittle they felt like they would snap in two.

"Where?" Jason whispered, stepping up behind Lorna.

"Straight up," she gasped, so intent on Gideon she hadn't heard Jason approach. "He says it's an old woman. I think he's still listening, trying to figure out exactly where she is. He knows the general vicinity, but hasn't pinpointed the exact spot."

Immediately, Jason shined a bright light up the mountainside and scanned back and forth until Gideon's form appeared in the beam. He wasn't far away—just a few meters. And he was still making his way upward, one deliberate step at a time. When the light hit him, he spun around and waved, but didn't say a word.

The one exception to the mandatory bedtime rule was when a rescue was in full swing. Everybody who was free came, including Frayne, whose camera light came on the instant he got to the spot where Lorna was standing, and doubled the light exposure to the rescue area. Then Harry, the other doctor with the group, appeared, as did Brian, the paramedic, and Tom, the nurse, who had left Gwen in his place in the hospital as she never went out on a rescue. There were also several local volunteers, all carrying lights. In the blink of an eye, the rescue site went from nearly pitch black and solitary to as light as day and bustling with activity.

"Was she responding to your voice?" Priscilla asked as she arrived. She had her dog, Philo, in tow. Philo was a black and white Belgian sheepdog—a gorgeous dog who was anxious to get off the leash and get to work. Max, in the grip of Jason, was also ready for the rescue.

Did the dogs feel the adrenaline of it, too? Lorna wondered, because there was a different feel in the air now. It was charged with pure, raw energy, and everybody, including Priscilla, who had looked exhausted only an hour ago, was alert and ready. "Not yet. We heard a whimper earlier, but she's been quiet since then. I'm getting a little nervous that—"

"Let the dogs come up," Gideon shouted. "It's stable enough."

Immediately Max and Philo were unleashed, and what Lorna saw after that was astonishing. Both dogs started their ascent, slowly at first, each one going in a different direction. Priscilla followed Philo and Gideon came around to walk abreast of Max. "Good boy," he said, then simply let the dog do what it wanted to do. Search. It took less than a minute for both dogs to find the object of their search, and Max let out a shrill yip as he bounded across a pile of house debris and stopped at what appeared to be a roof lying flat on the ground. Philo zoomed in at the same time and stayed there while Priscilla and Gideon hurried to catch up to the animals.

"Just so you'll know," Gideon shouted to Lorna, "that was the bark from Max that tells us somebody's alive."

From down below she watched as Gideon and Priscilla picked their way through the debris and finally came to the rooftop. Who would have thought to look underneath it? It was flush with the ground, almost buried in the dirt, and there was a lot of debris on top of it.

"Lorna!" Gideon called. "You and Tom come up top. Jason, there's nothing we can do here until morning, so take Max back and grab a couple hours of sleep."

Jason handed over a flashlight to Lorna, then she set out to follow Gideon up the face of the hill, passing Priscilla who was on her way back down with Philo. "I don't know what to say," Lorna commented in passing. "It happened so quickly."

"The dogs did in minutes what it might have taken us hours

to do." She gave her dog a pat on the head. "The first time I saw it happen I knew I had to have a dog."

"As far as I'm concerned, his status of dog just elevated to hero." Lorna also gave Philo a pat, then continued her way on up toward Gideon. "Oh," she called back, turning, "I want to do a special segment on just the dogs. Frayne...would you get some footage?"

When she arrived at the spot the dogs had located, Gideon was taking a hard look at the area in the very limited light available that far up the hill. "She's in there," he said. "But we can't get her out yet. It's going to take several people to get the roof off her, and I can't bring anybody else up here until we have a better look at the area. First thing in the morning, when we have more light. Tom, what I need for you to do is go back and get the medical supplies ready. Don't know her condition, but dehydration for sure, probably shock. Get yourself rested up because I want you up here when we lift the roof...want you to be the first one in."

Tom laughed. "Like I didn't see that coming."

"Tom's the athlete in the bunch. We take advantage of it," Gideon explained to Lorna.

"More like abuse it," Tom teased, giving Gideon a playful punch on the arm as he headed back to base camp.

"He's born for the work," Gideon commented. "Comes out on just about every rescue. Jason and I are thinking about grooming him to head up another unit in due time." He bent down, picked up a board, and tossed it aside. "Now, talk to her. Under better circumstances I'd get one of the locals up here to interpret, but one of our policies is that we don't put the local volunteers in danger, and until I can get a better look at the area, I can't have any of them coming up here."

"But you heard her again?" Lorna asked, still so overwhelmed at the speed by which this rescue was taking place she was nearly speechless.

"Heard her, and she responded to me. I've got to do some clearing to get a better idea of where she is now, so keep talking to her."

Lorna nodded, fully understanding the importance of mere words. "We're going to get you out of there," she said to the woman, and this time she did hear a response. The whimper turned into muffled words, and her heart lurched in her chest. Suddenly, it became urgent. She'd made the connection. She was the lifeline. "We're all here, and we won't go anywhere until we can find you," she promised. Then she stopped for a listen, her medical instincts taking over. "Words a little slurred and thick," she said.

"You can tell?" Gideon asked.

"It's hard to, since I don't speak the language. But there are speech patterns, and she's a bit sluggish. Probably dehydration and exhaustion. Hope it's isn't diabetes or a slight stroke. But she seems almost too alert for that."

"Damn, Lorn," he said, heading up the hill. "I'd forgotten how good you were at diagnosis. You listen to her for a minute and you can diagnose her. You always did have that gift."

"And the next thing you're going to tell me is what a waster I am, being on television instead of spending all my time in a medical practice." That was rather testy of her, but she wasn't comfortable with a compliment from Gideon. She always felt like the compliment came first and there was a big negative addendum to follow. *You always did have that gift, Lorna. Too bad you don't use it. Or, You always did have that gift, Lorna. And just how do you use it making your diagnosis on the telly?*

"Actually, I was going to tell you that you look pretty good on television. Got a good voice for it. Nice mannerisms. Useful information, at least what I've heard." With that, he disappeared into a clump of bushes, and continued his way around the scene, assessing it as best he could in the near darkness.

A real compliment from Gideon? And on top if it, he watched her? That was a bit of surprise. Not so much that he'd watched her, but that he'd admitted it. He'd refused to tune in when she'd been doing the local broadcast back when they'd been married. To her knowledge he'd never once seen her then. In fact, he d made a point of letting her know he wouldn't watch her.

So, should she tell him that when she'd had the chance, she'd watched news accounts of his work these past years? And that he had a good voice for the telly, too?

No, she decided. Some things were better left alone. Admitting that she'd watched him admitted to a sentiment she wasn't comfortable with. So instead of dwelling on anything to do with Gideon, she set about her task of talking to the trapped woman, and ten minutes later she was still talking when Gideon finally made his way back to Lorna. "Her name's Ana Flavia," she told him. Lorna was sitting on a piece of wall now, keeping herself out of the mud. "Her voice is a little stronger, still a bit thick, though. She's been asking for water."

"Wish we could get it to her."

"Wish we could just pick up the damned roof and get it off her," Lorna snapped.

Gideon dropped down next to her and gave her hand a squeeze. "We'll stay with her until morning. Then at first light, when we can make the proper evaluation on how to go about the rescue safely, we'll get her out."

"And there's nothing we can do until then?" she asked, even though she already knew the answer. Gideon was cautious, and he had to be. But sitting, doing nothing, was so difficult.

"It's not always easy, Lorn. Sometimes the waiting's the hardest part, especially when you're so close. But it never does any good to put others in danger, which is what we'd be doing if we tried getting her out now. We need daylight."

Lorn. He'd called her that earlier, and she'd almost forgotten that had been his pet name for her in their more casual moments. Lorna for proper, Lorn for everything else. "Well, I'll stay."

"You don't have to do that," Gideon said. "We've got plenty of others who can, and it's going to be a long night."

"Except she knows my voice, responds to me, and I know how it feels to want someone with you and not have them." Lorna scooted away from Gideon, already regretting that little dig at him. This was neither the time nor the place. Maybe there wasn't a time or place since it had happened so long ago, and they were no longer connected. But it had simply slipped out, and she did feel bad. "Look, I'm sorry. I didn't mean to say that."

"I deserved it," he said, his voice so flat she couldn't read anything into it.

"No, you don't. And I *am* sorry." The lights from the few volunteers below who'd remained on the scene followed Lorna as she stood up and made her way closer to the roof, one cautious step at a time. Oh, for the balance of a mountain goat, she thought as she tripped over a shattered chair, was nearly felled by a broken door, and banged her shin on a galvanized sink. Once there, fairly intact, she squatted down in the mud. "I'm not going away," she declared for both Ana Flavia's benefit, even though the woman didn't understand English, as well as Gideon's. "So I think I could use some of that nasty coffee right about now."

"Are you absolutely sure about this?" he asked. "I wanted you to have a firsthand look, but you don't have to get involved here."

"I'm involved, Gideon. I've been involved since the moment I stepped off the helicopter and I can't turn my back on it now."

"You're full of surprises tonight," he said.

"Maybe you wouldn't so surprised if you'd paid more attention to me when we were married. I've always been involved, Gideon. Just not in ways that suited you."

"You gave up a brilliant practice to go into television. How was I supposed to feel about that?"

"Happy for me because I'd found something I truly loved doing. And I didn't give up my practice. I just didn't work at it full time. In spite of what you've thought about me, Gideon, I'm still a doctor. I see patients, I direct care."

"But television comes first."

So he was still being judgmental. She'd thought maybe she'd noticed some change in him, some softening, or tolerance, but perhaps she was seeing only what she wanted to see, because this had been one of the arguments that led to the demise of their marriage. "My duty to my patients comes first, no matter where they are. That's the way it's always been, and, whether or not you want to admit it, what I do on television provides a service."

"And you diagnosed a woman's condition from only listening to her voice. You can't compare the two."

"No," she admitted. "I can't. But I don't have to. Just like you don't have to compare the surgical practice you gave up to your search-and-rescue operation. You were a brilliant general surgeon. One of the best. And how often do you get to use those skills?"

"OK, so maybe I overstepped a little in my opinion."

"You always did," she said quietly. It was amazing. They'd had this argument so many times, yet this time there was no zing to it. It was more an intellectual discussion than a back and forth with a punch. They had changed with time, it seemed. They were more mellow now. Maybe even more tolerant. Pity they couldn't have been like that five years ago. "So, how about that coffee? And maybe something to snack on. It looks like it's going to be a long night."

"OK, if that's what you want. We never leave them alone once we've found them but, like I said, we can spot you here. Trade off every hour."

"She trusts *my* voice, Gideon, " Lorna said. "I can't leave her."

As she spoke, the woman responded in words Lorna didn't understand, and that sealed it for her. She wasn't budging from that place until she was able to take the old woman with her. "So keep the coffee coming."

Down below on the path where a handful of rescuers and as many local volunteers had gathered, the lights continued to shine. And Frayne continued to film. But Lorna wasn't anxious to turn this into a scene in her documentary. So far, she wasn't anxious to turn anything into documentary footage. It was too intrusive, but more than that, in only a few hours, she'd come to feel like part of the team. The medical team, not the television team. Perhaps in the light of day she'd feel differently. Maybe she'd get her journalistic edge back when the sun came up. But until morning she was only a doctor, squatting in the mud, comforting a very frightened woman.

It was a nice feeling.

It was an even nicer feeling having Gideon by her side as she went through it.

CHAPTER FIVE

"It'll keep some of the rain off," Gideon said as he draped the rubber rain slicker over Lorna's shoulders.

She was sitting on a sheet of plastic now, drinking coffee and talking to the woman. They still wouldn't let the translator come up because of the precarious weather setting back in, but it was amazing how, when Ana Flavia didn't understand her and she didn't understand Ana Flavia, they'd formed a close bond in the past few hours. "I never realized how long the night could be," she said wearily, desperately fighting the urge to scoot a little closer to Gideon and lean her head against his shoulder. He hadn't made a gesture toward her, though, except covering her with the slicker, and as much as someone strong to lean on for a little while seemed nice, it wasn't going to happen. Not with Gideon.

"Neither did I, until the first time I was on a rescue that had to suspend the search until daylight. We were looking for a child lost in the woods. She was five. Her parents were on a picnic and didn't notice when she wandered off. By the time we were called in, it was late, maybe seven or eight hours after the local authorities had done their search and failed. It was almost dusk by then, but we set up the operation, laid out the grid, and just barely got started when they called off the search for the night because the area was too rough—ravines, wild animals. Too dangerous, they told us. I remember sitting up until daylight, drinking stale coffee like you're doing, thinking about all the things that could happen to the child, and cursing the night because we couldn't get out on the hunt for her. That was the longest night of my life."

"Did you find her in the morning?" Lorna asked.

"No," Gideon whispered. "Not alive, anyway. She'd fallen down one of those ravines, not too far off from where her family had picnicked. The coroner ruled she'd died instantly."

They were silent for a moment, Gideon lost in memories, Lorna feeling a deep sadness at his words. "Were we married then?" she eventually asked. "Because I don't recall your ever saying anything about it."

"No. It was after. I'd just quit the hospital and decided to go full time as a rescue doctor. And let me tell you, I almost changed my mind again after that, but a day later we went into a cave after an injured spelunker and saved his life, and that changed my mind again."

"What made you decide to make the switch from surgery? When we were married you said you were only going to do search and rescue on a part-time basis." Although the longer they'd been married, the longer part time had become. Finally, at the end, his surgical practice had become part time and his rescue pursuits had taken up most of his time.

"For starters, I liked it better than surgery. Even back when I was a student, and I wasn't allowed to do much more than basic first-aid, I loved going out and doing something most people would never see, or understand. Thinking about someone being trapped and injured, and alone…" He shook his head. "Like Ana Flavia… If we weren't here, she might never have been found. I mean, it's a big world out there and we do such a small part, but it's…"

"Important," Lorna offered.

"And fulfilling."

"I'm not surprised, really. I think I could see it coming when we were together. You were kind of like Max and the way he gets excited when he knows he has a live rescue spotted."

He chuckled. "Except I didn't bark like that."

"Maybe not bark, but it was the same thing. You couldn't wait to get out, and your regular surgery seemed more like it was passing time for you. I knew you weren't happy as a surgeon. Or not happy enough."

"You saw that?"

"Believe it or not, I did pay attention. Even when you were being a regular horse's rear end."

"As in being a horse's rear end about you accepting the television job?" he asked.

"About me accepting the television job," she confirmed.

"So why did you do it, Lorna? You never told me you were thinking about it. You just came home one day and flatly announced that's what you were going to do, then you did it. It was like my opinion didn't matter."

"It mattered, Gideon. But you wanted your opinion to be the only one in something that was my decision to make. You didn't want me to accept the position, and as far as you were concerned there was only your side to it. What I wanted didn't count. And maybe your opinion might have mattered more but you actually demanded that I quit. Demanded, Gideon! If I'd done the same with your rescue work, would you have? I mean, I did worry when you went off. It would have been easy for me to demand you quit, stay in your surgical practice, stay safe."

"You wouldn't have done that," he said stiffly.

"Which is the point. You shouldn't have. And you know what, Gideon? I liked what I was doing. Liked working part time at the television station and part time at the hospital. After my very first broadcast I got letters from people thanking me, telling me I'd made a difference. And you know what that first segment was about?"

"No, I never—"

"You never watched," she interrupted. "I remember. But others did, and on my first segment, when I talked about the symptoms of cervical cancer, I had three different readers write and tell me that because of what I'd said they'd recognized the symptoms in themselves, gone to their doctor, had the tests, had the diagnosis, and were on the road to recovery. Each one said I saved her life. And if three women who saw me wrote in, how many more who saw me and recognized the symptoms in themselves didn't write but got help?" She drew in a deep breath. "Public awareness is good medicine, whether or not you choose to admit that."

"Do you still like what you're doing?" he asked.

"I love it. From that very day until now, my feelings about what I do haven't changed."

"Then I'm glad you didn't listen to me," he said. "So how long after the divorce before you moved to New York?"

Well, that was certainly a peculiar thing to say. Not exactly an apology, but it was a step forward. "About six months. I was offered a network position on the morning news program. Five days a week. And an offer came through in a little hospital to go on staff as a hospitalist. Seemed like everything was falling into place for me, so I went. And that's where I've stayed. Happy, I might add. And you? How long before you gave up your surgery altogether?"

"Three months. No point in drawing it out. I quit the hospital three months later, moved to Texas to be nearer the base of operation, and that, as they say, is the end of the story."

"Except the part where you're in charge now. I'm impressed, Gideon. I know we had our difficulties, and I went through some strange things when I was pregnant…" Like extreme separation anxiety when her husband had been away. Like feelings of total inadequacy. Like she wanted to tell him how she was feeling, but couldn't. "But I'm glad you got what you wanted. This worked out well for you, and I'm impressed."

"You've changed," he said quietly. "You're more confident, assertive."

"We all do change, I suppose. Experience, time…it's bound to leave a few marks, hopefully for the better." It was good to get off the subject of her television career. They would never agree on it no matter how much fighting they did, and right now she just didn't want to fight. Didn't want to take a scalpel and open old wounds. Besides, her legs were beginning to tingle…going to sleep. So instead of saying anything else to Gideon that would, invariably, cause more argument—like, yes, she was more confident and assertive thanks to her career before the camera—Lorna stood and walked around for a minute. "Ana Flavia, are you OK?" she called out as she was trying to stomp some circulation back in.

Ana Flavia took a moment to respond, then amid the flurry of parched words, Lorna did hear, 'OK.'

"Her voice is weaker," she said to Gideon. "I'm getting concerned about her condition. I think she's been trapped for quite a while, maybe even since the beginning of all this, which would be over two days now. No food, no water, and God knows how old she is…" She shivered. "I don't know if we have until morning, Gideon." It was so damned frustrating being so close, yet in a very real sense so far away. "Can't we get more light up here and see if we can get her out? Or maybe somehow I could get in."

He stood too. "More light means more people. The ground's not stable, especially with all the rain that's come down in the past hour, and if we can't see what we're doing we could dislodge something that would kill her. I know it's frustrating, Lorn, but trust me. Her best shot is for us to wait until we can see the whole area."

"If the side of the mountain doesn't slide down on us in the meantime," Lorna snapped, angry at Gideon, angry over the situation, angry at herself for not being able to do more.

"That's always a possibility, and I do have people watching for that now." He pointed to several torchlights aimed at various positions up above them. "If it looks like it's going to slide, we'll do what we have to do."

"Are they all this dangerous?" Lorna asked. "All the rescues you go out on, are they all this dangerous?"

"Many of them, no. In the United States, we get call-outs quite often to search a forest for a lost child, and most of the time those are pretty safe…for the rescuers. But some call-outs are even worse than this. The ones I don't like the most are the coal mines after a cave in. I'm not a great fan of crawling on my belly in dark places, but more often than not that's what those turn out to be. And they're always unstable and unsafe."

"Yet you go in."

"Someone has to. Might as well be me. Besides, I never put my people in jeopardy if the risk is too great."

That wasn't even him trying to be the hero. It was Gideon putting everybody before himself. He broke the rules, he put himself at the greatest risk because that's the way he was. She wondered, briefly, if he would have been like that if they'd stayed married, had a family, built a life. Would he have ended up being a risk taker? "All the time we were together, I didn't know the details," she said, picking up her Thermos of coffee and pouring a little into the cup lid. After taking a sip, she handed it to Gideon. "I knew what a rescue operation was, but I always pictured you doing the medical treatment more than anything else. Kind of like what Gwen does. You did that on purpose, didn't you? Not telling me everything?"

"It kept you from worrying."

"I would have worried, Gideon. God, I would have worried. But I had the right to know, the right to worry. And you didn't allow me that." Even though they weren't married now, something told her she would worry in the future now that she knew.

"You mean like you didn't allow me into your decision when you decided to change career directions? I had a right to know that, Lorna, before you signed the contract. Before you went and changed our life together without even telling me."

For a brief moment, both were quiet. It was as if an unspoken reality was slipping down over them. Something she couldn't define, but something she definitely felt. Lorna shivered, not from the chill of the rain, but from the cold realization that she and Gideon should have been better together the first time and that the end of their marriage hadn't been as one-sided she'd convinced herself it had been.

But she and Gideon had been married, and perhaps, if she'd given him a chance before she'd made her decision, his opinions wouldn't have turned into demands. Too late to know. One thing was sure, though. They'd both suffered their fair share of marital maladjustments. Only now she was coming to realize her own part in the breakdown.

"Well, you're right about the coffee," he finally said, breaking the disquieting moment between them as he handed the cup back to Lorna. "If the mud slides don't kill us, the coffee will."

"So why didn't we ever talk about it?" she asked. "Was it something that simply slipped into a habit for us, ignoring what was really happening?"

"I was just asking myself the same question," he said.

"And?"

"And I don't know. I'd like to say we were too young and let it go at that, but we weren't. We were both nearly thirty, me just over, you just under, so that's not an excuse. Anything else just makes us seem…"

"Pathetic," she supplied.

Chuckling, he stretched his arms over his head, then stretched his back, trying to work out the kinks setting in. "I was thinking something more like a match made in hell from the beginning, but too good in bed to notice that everything else was falling apart. Could you rub my neck just a minute…a little on the left side?"

Sex had been their way of avoiding the things they hadn't wanted to face. It had been easier that way. Go to bed, make love, forget about everything else.

Suddenly, a slight smile crept to Lorna's face as she turned to give him a little massage. They'd spent an awful lot of time avoiding things and Gideon was right, they'd been positively brilliant at that aspect of their marriage. A wistful sigh replaced the smile, though. Positively brilliant, and not in a way they should have been. "We did have our moments, though," she conceded, finding the tight spot…the spot that had always been tight every time he'd asked her to do this.

"And some of them actually mattered," he murmured, sounding a little like a contented big cat.

But too many of them hadn't, which was what had killed them. Try as she might, Lorna couldn't remember very many moments that had mattered. In a three-year relationship from beginning to end, her memories should have been full to overflowing. "I'm sorry we were who we were. And you're right. Some of the moments did matter, just not enough."

"No regrets, Lorna. Things work out they way they're meant to—good, bad or otherwise." Gideon leaned back slightly as she moved her massage down over his shoulder. "In spite of the way it turned out, I don't regret our marriage. And for what it's worth, I'm sorry for my end of the problems. I know I caused my share of them."

"You've never said anything like that before," she said. Maybe he had changed after all.

He chuckled. "At the time, it was *all* your fault. But I've had five years to think about it, to shift the pieces of the puzzle, and I've seen some things differently."

Which ones? she wondered. "I'm sorry, too. I made mistakes…"

"Lorna?" Ana Flavia called out, breaking up the moment.

"OK?" Lorna called back.

"OK," she responded.

"She's getting weaker. Beginning to give out, I think." She stopped the massage when her urge was to go on down his forearm. Bad idea. She remembered where it went from there. Over the arm, across the abdomen, then on down...Very bad idea! "Without any fluids in her for so long, I'm concerned about kidney damage."

He snapped away from her when she stopped, probably remembering the same thing she had. "She's probably fighting exhaustion. It happens. They fight with everything they've got when the search is on, calling for someone to find them, or trying to dig their way out. Then, when rescue is imminent, they give out."

"Will she make it?" Lorna asked. "In your experience, will Ana Flavia survive until morning?"

"People are resilient. They bounce back in amazing ways...ways you'd never expect them to."

"Then maybe I should let her sleep and save her strength, instead of disturbing her every couple of minutes. It's just that I don't want her to feel like I've abandoned her."

"As long as she hears your voice out here, she'll know she's not alone."

Like she'd so desperately wanted to hear his voice and not feel alone the day she'd miscarried.

The rain was beginning to pick up, and Lorna pulled the slicker up over her head. "So we wait," she said, her own voice shaky. "For as long as it takes."

"As long as it takes," he repeated. He pulled into his slicker too, and now there were merely two rubber bundles huddled on the side of a muddy slope, waiting for the first light of day. Lots of problems out in the open, lots of problems still tucked away. Even so, there was no one in the world she'd rather be doing this with other than Gideon. "So tell me all about Houston," she finally said. In truth, she wanted to know…wanted to know so much more than she dared ask.

"For starters, I live in a warehouse that serves as the offices and equipment storage facility for Global Response. Nice apartment. Lots of space." He chuckled. "Most of it empty since I don't need much other than my job."

"How did you hook up with them? I thought you were with On Call Rescue."

"That's who I was with when we were married. But one of the guys I'd worked with there went out on his own and set up this unit. I went with him to be his assistant in charge. Then he was…"

Gideon's voice trailed off, and Lorna held her breath, already anticipating what he would say when he spoke again. "Killed?" she asked hesitantly.

"Married," he said. "Moved to Switzerland with his wife. Turned the company over to me."

Lorna breathed a sigh of relief. Sure, death was a possibility in this kind of work. But tying it to Gideon in a very real sense…she was relieved that she didn't have to.

"They're running a mountain rescue operation out of a village clinic together," he continued.

"And happy, like Jason and Priscilla?" She didn't know why she cared, but she did. Maybe it was because she was still surprised that a married couple could survive that kind of a situation, and even thrive in it. Deep down, she was a little envious.

"Happy, starting a family, having all the good things they deserve."

Lorna straightened her back, and shifted positions from cross-legged to legs straight out. They poked out from under the slicker, but it didn't matter. Wet was wet, and she couldn't get any wetter than she already was. "And you got your own search-and-rescue operation. That's what you always wanted, wasn't it?"

"Something like that," he said. "Look, I'm going to go back down and make sure everything is good to go come sun-up. Will you be OK here by yourself for about ten minutes?"

She'd been OK by herself for the entirety of their marriage, then all the years afterwards. So ten minutes one way or another didn't really make much of a difference at all. Still, when he'd gone, she did feel a little lonely.

"They're on their way up," Gideon shouted from his spot adjacent to the pile of debris imprisoning Ana Flavia. Kneeling in the mud, he was meticulously removing the boards, one at a time, trying to get to her, while Lorna was relegated to the scene below, where the others had stood with their torches last night. She was near the rescue in progress, but not allowed in now. It made sense as she wasn't experienced in this, but she so wanted to be up there to help.

It was good watching Gideon, though…watching him in his element. She'd never seen this before, and a new sense of respect was welling up in her for what he did. This was only one incident, and he did this time and time again, day in, day out. He experienced the highs and the lows, then picked himself up and started all over again wherever he was needed. Yes, she did respect that, and him. More than that, she was in awe. Imagine that! In awe of her ex-husband. Well, stranger things had been known to happen, she supposed. Five years ago she hadn't cared if she never saw him again and now he was at the top of her most-admired list.

Lorna twisted to look at the other volunteers making their way up the mountain face. She admired them, too. All of them.

"Are you holding up?" Tom asked, as he brushed by her.

"I'll be holding up better once you get her out."

"Shouldn't take long," he promised, as he continued upward. Jason was there, along with Brian, a couple of the other volunteers who'd come down with Gideon, and a whole host of locals. True to his word, Gideon allowed the experienced up while everybody else stayed down below, carting off debris that had been pulled away, fetching water for the rescuers, standing at the ready for anything necessary. And for the next two hours it was a dreadfully slow, nerve-racking process getting in to Ana Flavia. But the crew was methodical about it, and cautious. So Lorna stood by with the rest of them, going as far as permitted to receive an armload of debris, taking an occasional drink of water up to the line, bandaging a few cuts and scrapes caused by the wood being pulled off Ana Flavia's prison, and mostly waiting. Finally, after what seemed to take as long as the endless night had, Gideon waved Lorna up. "Lorna," he called. "I think there's someone here you'd like to meet."

As she scrambled up the mountain face, slipping and sliding in the mud, the last thing on her mind was the way she looked, and how Frayne was filming every last scrap of the rescue. All she wanted was to see Ana Flavia...alive.

"How much longer?" she asked breathlessly, as she reached Gideon's side.

He smiled. "Not much."

"Is someone in there with her?"

"Tom went in about five minutes ago."

"And?"

"And he says she's weak, dehydrated, but she's doing fine. Her vital signs are holding, weak but not alarming, and she's alert. Asking for you."

"Thank God," Lorna whispered, a wave of pure relief washing over her just as Tom emerged from a hole cut down into the roof, helping Ana Flavia out with him. She was actually walking. Not steady on her feet, leaning heavily against Tom, but walking. And smiling.

Without asking, Lorna ran to the old lady and threw her arms around her. Ana Flavia collapsed in Lorna's arms, weeping and thanking her, and Lorna held onto her until Gideon signaled the stretcher up. Even then, she didn't let go of Ana Flavia's hand as they carried the stretcher back down to the trail then on to the base camp. And both women chatted the whole time, neither one understanding the other. But never mind. In those dark hours, the bond had formed, and Gideon was right. The words spoken didn't matter.

The rain had stopped an hour ago, and now only a light mist fell over the area. In the gray of the morning it looked ugly. And sad. But Ana Flavia was well, taking liquids nicely and soon to be allowed solid food, and Lorna was so relieved that even the dreary pall cast over the area didn't faze her. It was hard to believe that in another few hours she'd be on her way back home. But that was the case. Frayne had his footage, and in spite of all her medical activity she had her notes. This was a wrap, as they said. Time to go back to her real world. And in a bright sense, the sooner she got this documentary to air, the sooner donations would come in to support Gideon's operation. That was the ultimate end, the logical conclusion, her part of the bargain. And something this group of rescuers so desperately needed.

Still, she couldn't totally shake off the glum feeling sliding down over her. It was like something here wasn't yet finished. Her work as a doctor? Or as a media personality? Perhaps something with Gideon?

Lorna sighed, looking down the row of patients in the hospital tent. They were still coming in and going out and, in all honesty, her presence there wouldn't make much difference one way or another. Gideon's people were a very responsible bunch. They worked harder than any people she'd ever seen, cared deeply, and never complained. They deserved to have their story told. And soon.

"So do you need coverage in the hospital?" she asked Gwen, who whisked by her, carrying an IV set-up.

Gwen gave her a skeptical look before she answered. "I think Harry and Jason have both tents covered pretty well. But thanks." She scurried another few steps, then spun back. "But if you're looking for something to do right now, Dani and Tom went up to the south face. Tom didn't stock up his kit after the last rescue. Could you take a fresh medical bag out to him? Maybe when you get there, they'll let you join their search."

Well, that was some progress, wasn't it? She'd rather have been asked out on rescue where the primary goal for her wasn't to merely tote out some supplies, but people here didn't quibble. Everything was toward the same end. And maybe, just maybe, she wouldn't get back in time to catch the transport out.

That thought brought a smile to Lorna's face as she grabbed up a rucksack and radio and headed out the hospital tent door.

She looked exhausted, Gideon thought. Completely spent. But Lorna wasn't used to this kind of work. Her world was about primping for the camera, then smiling. Not breaking her finger-nails ripping at boards to rescue an old woman. Lorna had done such a good job last night, though, and he'd gained a new respect for her. He'd always known she was a good doctor, but her sheer will to save Ana Flavia had shown him a side of her he'd never seen. Or never been around to see. He had to admit though, he had been surprised by her determination to see the rescue through to the end.

Maybe it had always been there and he'd simply missed it. "Like I missed a lot of things," he said to Ana Flavia, who didn't understand a word he said. "I wasn't a very good husband, you know. I was always off doing what I wanted, and then when she had the opportunity to do what she wanted..." He cringed, thinking about it. "I tried to stop her, Ana Flavia. I tried to stop Lorna."

At that mention of Lorna's name, Ana Flavia's face lit up. "Lorna OK," she said.

"She sure is," Gideon agreed. "More than I ever noticed." Because he'd niched her into the same group as his parents the instant she'd become a journalist. To him, journalist equated to family neglect, instability, problems. "Lorna sure is OK, isn't she?" he said, almost wistfully.

Of all things, he was actually thinking about asking her to stay on to the end of this rescue. Maybe he should. Normally, he might have. But her cameraman, Frayne, was perpetually complaining that they'd been using up too much of Lorna's time with medical duties that weren't hers to perform. Which was true. They had been. She was willing, she was good. And if he didn't miss his guess, she liked the work. Of course the documentary was important to the operation. So it was probably best to let her get back to her own duties. Still, as he looked down at Ana Flavia's expectant face while he did a quick check now that she was settled into bed and adequately rehydrated, he wanted to ask Lorna to stay. That was personal, though. Not professional.

"Lorna OK," Ana Flavia said again, as Gideon prepared to take a few stitches in a gash on her arm. She smiled up at him.

Gideon returned the smile. "Yes," he whispered. "She is." More OK than he'd remembered her to be.

On her way up the trail, Lorna saw Estella's mother carry the child away. It was so good to see a happy ending here. Mother and daughter reunited. Estella's mother was crying, hugging her daughter tight. In the end, that's all that mattered, really. Not the houses. Not the possessions. Just the lives, the reunions. "I'm glad there are happy endings," Lorna said to Estella's mother in passing, even though the woman didn't understand. But she understood Lorna's smile, because she offered one back.

"No, you can't stay," she said to herself as she made her way through the mud. "Don't even think about it. This is Gideon's life, not yours." But she was thinking about it…thinking hard as she took the hike up to the south face of the mountain. It was a lengthy one, and trying to get herself over all the remains of houses and other buildings washed out by the mud and rain was difficult. It wasn't raining now, but what had come down overnight and first thing that morning had made the area even slicker than it had been yesterday, and Lorna was forced to choose her steps deliberately so she didn't fall down.

Overall, the area was beautiful, though. The jungles lush and green, the mountains stunning. It was no wonder that only a few kilometers down the road several lavish resorts had nestled themselves into the countryside to play host to the wealthy who traveled in from the entire of Rio de Janeiro State and São Paulo, and from as far away as Goiânia and Brasilia, to holiday in luxury unequaled by anything else in this part of the world. The air here was refreshing and not so humid for a subtropical climate. The temperatures were moderate, too. Not as hot as the summer's hottest temperatures, and not as cold as the winter's coldest.

It was a perfect place in so many ways, yet when the rains came… Lorna shuddered, looking up the south face of the mountain. When the rains came, nothing was perfect.

"Dani," she said into the radio, hoping the reception would be good. There were too many people scattered about, picking through their belongings, to find her amongst them. "Dani, it's Lorna. Can you hear me?"

Dani's radio crackled on. "I thought you were working down at the hospital."

"All the other doctors were down there, so they didn't need me there."

"Good, because I could sure use a doctor up here. Dag wants to get on the trail, Tom's wandered off, and I have six people who need treating. Can't leave them alone as a couple have some significant injuries, but I need to let Dag loose because I think he's sensing a survivor somewhere close by."

"Tell me where you are and I'm on my way!" Lorna could almost feel the adrenaline starting to pump. Amazing, how much she liked this. So much of the time she'd been married, especially toward the end, she'd resented the way Gideon had always gone off at a moment's notice. They'd called, he'd run. But she understood that now. More than that, she owed him an apology.

Dani's directions were fairly easy to follow, and Lorna found her within minutes. "Dag's frantic," she said, pointing to her German Shepherd, a typical tri-color variety. "He wants to get off leash, and get on the hunt, and when's he's this anxious I hate to hold him back." She turned an affectionate smile toward her dog. "These dogs…it's amazing how much they want to help. Look, I'm going to catch up with Tom. He has a couple of the volunteers with him further up but I'll send one back to you, if you want."

Lorna took a quick appraisal of the casualties awaiting treatment, all six men and women sitting and lying on muddy boards ripped out from the houses. They were all conscious, all alert, and none seemed too much in pain. "I'll be fine here," she said, dropping the bag of medical supplies onto one of the boards.

Dani held up her two-way radio as she untied Dag's leash from a small palm tree. "If you need me…"

Lorna nodded, as she turned her attention to her first patient. She was glad to be doing this. Maybe part of that was her need to show Gideon that she was just as much a doctor as he, that she could do the hard work, too. But the bigger part of it was that getting back into real hands-on medicine felt good. It had been a long, long time, and surprisingly she'd missed it. Missed it a lot. Sure, she was a hospital consultant, but her patient care was limited, and rarely ever in a hands-on capacity. She carried a clipboard, not a stethoscope. She made arrangements, not diagnoses. Such a vast world of difference in what she did there and what she was doing here. In a way, she envied Gideon his work. A week ago she would have argued rather adamantly that she was completely happy with what she did, but now, deep down, she thought she might be even happier doing the work Gideon did. It was fulfilling in a way she'd never felt in medicine since she'd left direct patient care. And that was as much a shock as her new, more mellow feelings toward her ex.

Such a huge difference in just a few hours and it was already clear that in the near future she was going to have to have a serious think over her career direction. Until then, being needed like this was gratifying, and before she left she was going to thank Gideon for the opportunity. "I know you probably can't understand me," she said as she bent down to her patient, a man near her own age, "but my name is Lorna, and I'm a doctor. Where are you hurting? *Meu nome é Lorna e eu sou um doutor. Onde você está frindo?*" One of the few Brazilian Portugese phrases she had learned on the way down, and she was glad she had.

Somehow in the back of her mind, though, she did wish that Gideon would happen along to see what she was doing. It was a sentiment that didn't make too much sense to her, wanting his approval. Or attention. But, honestly, nothing about her relationship with him had ever made sense. Not at the beginning, not at the end, not now. So why should this make any more sense than anything else?

Taking a quick glance over her shoulder just in case he might be coming along, Lorna forced off her disappointment with a good hard look at the task at hand when she saw that he wasn't, setting her mind solely on taking care of the six people right here who needed her.

Even so, Gideon was still in the back of her mind.

CHAPTER SIX

"GOOD shot," Frayne called up the hill to Lorna from his vantage point on the muddy trail just below. "Think you can turn yourself a little more toward the camera so I can get a better angle of your face?"

She knew he was only doing his job, but this did annoy her. So far, she'd splinted a broken ankle, butterflied a head gash, bandaged various cuts, and now she was evaluating a woman with chest pains. Broken ribs, she suspected. And panic. Enough to cause huge chest pains. But she wanted to make sure it wasn't something more serious, and the last thing she needed was to do it for a better camera angle.

Pulling a stethoscope out of the rucksack, Lorna popped the earpieces in and had a listen. Juniata's heart was racing a little, but not badly. And it was steady. Her lungs sounded good, her skin color was fine. But over her mid-section, below her sternum and to the right, was a huge bruise—one as large as a dinner plate and a deep, angry red. Lorna cringed, nearly feeling the pain herself, as she ran her fingers lightly over the area. Without an X-ray it was hard to tell what was going on internally, but anything that caused that kind of bruising had, most likely, broken something. Broken ribs at the worst, torn cartilage at the best. Either way, she didn't have what was necessary for a decent splint, so Juniata would have to go to base camp, along with João and his broken ankle. The others could go along home, if they still had homes. Or they'd be welcomed at base for a hot meal and a bed.

"Lorna," Frayne shouted. "Did you hear me? I need a better shot of you."

"This is the best I can do," she yelled, not budging from her position, crouching in the mud alongside her patient. "I've got injured people up here and I can't maneuver around to accommodate the camera."

Dani had checked in briefly once, and said she was on her way up to the top of this particular face. It wasn't such a steep climb, and she'd told Lorna that Tom was already up there with volunteers, combing the area. They'd pulled three people from a half-collapsed structure so far, none of them injured badly enough to need medical attention, but one of them had mentioned a small one-room school further up. So Tom had gone on ahead, Dani was on her way, and Lorna intended to follow as soon as she finished here.

"Look, Lorna. We're running out of time if we want to meet deadline," Frayne yelled. "You've had your fun playing doctor, but we need to get back on schedule if we want to get out of here, get these tapes edited, and on air for the weekend."

To meet their deadline. Well, that was certainly her existence these days, wasn't it? Not a medical deadline. An on-air deadline. That had been the plan when she'd come to Brazil—grab the footage, get out. But she'd never expected this—not the sheer magnitude of what had happened here. The entire face of the mudslide went on for kilometers, some areas worse than others. And it was so odd…small patches of houses and cottages were left totally unscathed, with little old women sweeping the mud off their front porches, while the structure next door was totally flattened. Then across the way there was a patch of jungle with verdant vegetation and beautiful red, green and yellow parrots sitting unconcerned in the limbs, basking in the midday sun and looking across to the destruction. No rhyme or reason. It was a miracle anybody had gotten out, but so far, from everything she'd seen on her way out there, everybody had, and the casualty count was low, comparatively.

And people simply picked up and started over. That was the most amazing part. Already, the building process had commenced in many places…had commenced before the weather front was over. More rain was predicted, more mud inevitable, and the astonishing people of the area went about their daily lives. Of course, there was destruction here beyond the loss of human life, and in a sense, that's where the greatest toll might be measured. The people were so resourceful, though. She'd gone through a simple divorce which had thrown her off tilt for more months than she cared to count, and yet these people literally crawled out and started over, barely missing a beat.

It did give Lorna pause to think about some of the trifles in her world. Three days ago she'd nearly had a panic attack because her hair had been a little frizzy before she'd had to go on air, and she hadn't been able to find her styling gel. Today, the cakes of mud, straw, and who knew what else clinging to her hair didn't matter in the least. "Just shoot the best way you can," she called to her partner. "You can come in closer, get me any way you like, just don't get my patient."

"Even from your rear?" Frayne called.

The absolute rule—never from the rear. Out here it seemed silly. "Anywhere," she yelled, then rose up on her knees and waved to one of the local volunteers she recognized. He was running down the wash, slipping and sliding in his haste, and Lorna hoped he understood enough English to get her patients back to the hospital.

"Trapped!" he shouted, when he was finally in earshot of her. "Come fast!"

"Who? Where?" she called, standing up.

The young man pointed up to the area where Dani was headed. "Hurt. Hurt bad."

They'd found casualties! Children in the collapsed school? That was Lorna's first thought as she shouted to Frayne. "I need you to stay here with my two patients until we can get them back to the hospital. Will you do that for me?"

For a moment, the look that crossed his face caused her to doubt that he would, but finally he lowered the camera from his shoulder and shrugged. Then he began the climb up the hillside as Lorna began her own climb to higher ground, dreading what she would find once she was there.

"Casualties," she called into her radio as she started upward.

"Lorna?" the voice on the other end crackled back.

"We have a school, Gideon. Don't know the extent of damage, but I'm on my way up. Frayne's down below. He'll show you where we are."

"No!" he shouted. "Lorna, wait until we get to you!"

By the time those words were out, the radio was tucked into her pocket and she was fighting against the slick mud on her way to the rescue.

Gideon didn't doubt her medical skills, but he didn't know her rescue skills and that was the problem. They never let any inexperienced volunteers out to do what he feared Lorna was about to do, and half of him wanted to strangle her for doing something so stupid, while half of him wanted to hug her for doing something so brave. Lorna Preston was an amazing woman. Lorna Preston Merrill had been an amazing woman, too, only he'd been too blind to see it. "Send up a team!" he shouted to Priscilla on his way out of the hospital tent. "Don't know what we've got yet. She didn't say."

One of his trained rescuers would have said more. Exact

location. Condition of the area. One of his trained rescuers would have set out with a partner. "Damn," he muttered. Mud splashed up to his knees as he ran down the trail, carrying a sackful of supplies in one hand and a radio in the other. "Lorna," he shouted into it, his voice breathy. "Come in, Lorna."

No answer.

"Dani, are you out there?"

No answer again.

This wasn't good. "Tom?"

Again, nothing. Not one of his people was answering. Cardinal rule, keep in touch! The first thing that crossed his mind was that it was time for a refresher course on protocol. Even the best, including himself, needed reminding, and he was a prime example of breaking the rules as he was out on his own. No partner. Yes, a refresher course would be good, and he made a mental note to schedule it. But then the second thing raced through his mind, and a cold chill gripped him. Other than breaking protocol, or simply losing a radio, which might happen to one of his people, but not two of them together, like Dani and Tom were, the only other reason for no one to answer was…"Damn," he muttered, picking up his pace. That was a reason he didn't even want to think about.

He also didn't want to think about Lorna, out there alone, heading into *that* possibility.

The higher Lorna and the volunteer went, the steeper it got, and by the time Lorna was near the top of this particular wall of mud, she was practically crawling her way through it on her hands and knees. So far, she hadn't seen anybody up there except a handful of people picking through the remains of their houses. No one was injured and, thank God, no one was dead. But there were more damaged and destroyed buildings ahead, and no way of knowing what she'd find when she reached the next level up, or the one after that. "Remind me to switch to a first-floor flat when I go home," she muttered, taking a brief pause to brush a twig out of her hair. It had caught fast and scratched her cheek.

"Lorna Preston!" someone ahead shouted. She looked up in time to see one of the volunteers from camp, not one of the local volunteers, frantically waving at her. "Over here. We need help!"

That's all it took to get her going again. One thing was sure— she wasn't even close to being in the good physical shape she'd thought she was. The work was hard, the effort to climb up the side of the hill exhausting. By the time she'd reached her destination on the shelf above, she was so winded her belly hurt and her chest felt on fire. So maybe she understood more now why, years ago, Gideon had always collapsed when he'd come home from a rescue—collapsed and sometimes stayed in bed, sleeping, for two days straight. She'd always been so glad to see him, and hurt that all he'd wanted to do was sleep when she'd wanted to make up for the time he'd spent away. Even the sexy little nighties she'd bought for his homecomings hadn't worked at those particular times.

Yes, now she understood, and felt a little embarrassed. What she didn't understand, though, was how she could have listened to him tell her about his rescues and yet never truly heard. Another apology she owed him. One of the many adding up lately.

"What is it?" she asked the volunteer.

"I think Tom McCain's down. Haven't heard from him in ten minutes. So is Dani." This was another of the four U.S. volunteers from Gideon's team—the one called Richard Eggington. He was a computer programmer, Lorna had heard. No medical experience, but he came out to do the hard labor whenever he had a chance. "Dani's in a lot of pain. Don't know a thing about Tom. He's off the radio and I've got a couple of the locals looking for him, so as soon as you can get to Dani, I'm going back up to help look and make sure the volunteers aren't getting into any difficulty."

"What…happened?" Lorna gasped, trying to catch her breath.

"School structure. We were on our way in to have a look and it partially collapsed." He took hold of Lorna's arm and pulled her along until she finally found Dani, lying in the mud at the edge of a pile of splintered wood and timbers, on her back, eyes closed, breathing labored. "Tom had gone around to the rear by himself and Dani was on her way in the front to make a safety determination. She was just beginning to access the entry, not even inside, and it fell. When it did, I couldn't drag her away and risk more injury, but I got the beams off her."

"Dani," Lorna said, dropping down next to her. "Can you tell me where it hurts?"

"Pelvis," she managed. "Legs." She bit her lip and sucked in a sharp breath. "Back."

Lorna immediately felt for a pulse. Weak and thready. Dani was also cold and pale. "Does it hurt to breathe?" she asked.

"Breathing's OK. Find Dag. Please, find Dag."

Lorna looked up at Richard, who shrugged. "We'll take care of him," she whispered, as she gently pulled back Dani's eyelids for a look. Everything there was fine, no apparent head trauma. But after taking a blood-pressure reading…it was so low it was almost not readable. And Dani's belly…what had been flat was now distended, and tight. Internal bleeding!

"Tell Tom I didn't find anybody," Dani managed. "Not in the front part. Didn't get in, though. Maybe he'll have better luck from the rear…" She took in a breath, coughed, and shuddered. "Tell him to find Dag," she choked.

"But Tom—" Lorna started to say. Richard laid a warning hand on her shoulder before she could finish, though, and Lorna instantly understood. Dani didn't know Tom was missing. "As soon as he comes back down," Lorna continued, "I'll tell Tom as soon as he comes back down."

"Is it bad?" Dani asked. She gasped and shuddered again as

a stab of pain shot through her, then she reached for Lorna's hand. "Am I going to…?"

"It's bad, but you're going to be fine." Lorna kept hold of Dani's hand, and with her other hand ran her fingers lightly over Dani's muddy slacks. Thank God there was no bone protruding. That much was good. If her legs were broken, which they probably were, at least the breaks were closed, and there was no risk of infection. She did the same exam for Dani's pelvis. To the touch, there was nothing to discover. But touch didn't diagnosis a fracture, and Lorna suspected that, like Dani's legs, her pelvis was also fractured as it had taken the brunt of the blunt force from the falling wood. "Can you wiggle your toes for me?" she asked, motioning for Richard to remove Dani's shoes. When he did, Lorna finally had to let go of Dani's hand to rummage though the medical kit to see what kind of painkiller she had in there. For Dani, the trip out of there would be as brutal as the injury itself, and without a little something to take the edge off, she was afraid Dani would go into shock. With internal bleeding, that could well prove to be fatal.

"I don't think I'm paralyzed," Dani forced out. The effort in her voice was becoming more pronounced as the minutes passed. "I still feel some movement…" She braced herself, bit her lips, and moved both her ankles in circles.

"Good," Lorna whispered.

"But I'm not going to dance any time soon?" Dani whispered, fighting to stay brave as the pain was increasing. "Tom will be disappointed. He promised to take me dancing in Rio once we get out of the mud."

Lorna glanced up at Richard just as he bit his lower lip and shut his eyes. "I think you're going to be watching the dancing for a while," she said.

Dani's injury was finally coming down on her now, and her eyes were fluttering shut. "Tell Tom to take care of Dag," she whispered. "Tell him I still want that dance he promised."

"Can you take morphine?" Lorna asked.

Dani didn't answer, so Lorna gave her a gentle shake. "Dani," she said. "Morphine?"

Dani nodded, and let out an exhausted breath.

She was gone for a while, but maybe it was for the best, Lorna thought as she drew the liquid from the vial and gave Dani the shot. There wasn't much else to do there, and if she did wake up, the morphine wouldn't take away all the pain, but it would help. "We need transport to get her out," she told Richard, "And she's going to need an airlift to the nearest trauma center, stat. Internal bleeding and other injuries. We don't have a lot of time." She reached to take Dani's pulse, then looked up at him. "What about Tom?"

"He was on the other side of the building when it went down. That's all I can tell you." He twisted, and waved. "Gideon!" he shouted. "Up here."

Gideon was on his way? Lorna spun around, glad to see him trudging up the muddy trail. "She's bad, but stable enough for transport," she said once he'd reached them. "Internal bleeding, crushed pelvis, possible legs. We need to get her out of here right away."

He looked at the collapsed school, and didn't ask what happened. "Tom?"

Richard shrugged. "Haven't seen him for a while. He was on the back side."

Gideon bent down and took Dani's hand. "We've got the team on the way up right now, and we'll have you out of here in just a little while. You hold on, Dani. You hear me? You hold on." As he said the words, Brian rushed up the trail. "You and Lorna get her back," Gideon said to him. "Richard and I will join up with Tom."

"I'm not going back," Lorna said stubbornly. "And don't pull rank, Gideon. I'm not part of your team." She understood why he wanted to send her back—the next minutes were critical and she wasn't trained like the others were—but she didn't agree. This was her rescue, she wanted to see it through.

Instead of arguing, Gideon merely nodded. "Fine. But you do what I tell you to. It's not negotiable, Lorna."

Before she could reply, he'd signaled Richard to help Brian take Dani down, then started up and around to the rear of the collapsed structure. By the time she caught up with him, Gideon had stopped and was simply staring at the remains. No sign of Tom. No sign of Dag. "Tom!" he yelled. "Tom, can you hear me?"

"Would he go in by himself?" Lorna asked. Gideon would have, but Tom?

"Yeah, he would. He reminds me a lot of—"

"You?" she interrupted.

"Unfortunately." His voice was oddly flat as he pulled out his radio. "Priscilla, bring up the dogs," he said, then turned to Lorna. "I'm going up higher to take a look around. I don't have a good vantage point here, and there's a possibility Tom did see something further up that he went after. Stay here, OK? Scout the immediate area, keep in contact. And, Lorn, don't take any risks." He bent forward and gave her a light kiss on her muddy, scratched cheek. "Because in that regard, you remind me of me, too." He signaled one of the volunteers over to accompany him, and started his upward climb.

"You take care, too, Gideon," she called after him.

Lorna watched as he continued up the face of the mountain, then when he'd disappeared over a knoll, she called one of the volunteers to join her—the one called Monty. Together, they started to search the area. "Tom! Can you hear me? Can you give me some indication of where you are?"

Nothing. So while Monty moved around to the side, Lorna moved closer to rear of the collapsed structure. Called. Listened. Nothing, again. "Monty, anything?"

"Nothing!" he replied.

She'd hoped, but…well, maybe Tom hadn't gone inside. Or maybe, unlike last night when she'd spent the night sitting with

Ana Flavia, who'd been talkative, he couldn't respond or wasn't in a place where she could hear him. She refused to think about the scenario fighting to fill her mind. Slowly, Lorna made her way around the perimeter of the fallen structure, looking, listening, hoping for any sign of life in the heap of tangled, broken wood. When she came up to the far side and met up with Monty who'd made his way around, she saw a large gap between the ground and the debris. Large enough to crawl through. Or at least, large enough to wedge herself into the opening and call again. "What do you think?" she asked him.

"I think we wait for Gideon."

Logical, but frustrating. Too much time wasted, especially if Tom was in a critical situation. Without so much as a thought about it, Lorna dropped to her knees, then flat on her belly, and wiggled into the dark hole, pushing her medical kit along in front of her. "Tom," she called, only a few feet in. "Help is on the way. If you can hear me…"

"Lorna!" Gideon yelled from behind, on his way back to the site. "It's not secured."

"And I'm not going in all the way." She turned to look at him. "He wouldn't have wandered so far away, Gideon," she said. "This was where he was searching. Not any place else. He's got to be in here!"

"I know."

Gideon sounded despondent, and the pain in those two words was so evident her heart clutched. The reality here wasn't good. Gideon knew it. She knew it. And the group of volunteers mixed with Gideon's team, all of them making their way up to the area to join in the search now, knew it. "Then you know somebody's got to go in. I'm the only one who's small enough, except Priscilla, and she needs to be out with Philo."

"I know that, too. But you're not qualified."

"And you're not going to stop me, are you? Put yourself in my place, Gideon. What would *you* do?"

He shook his head, then dropped to his knees behind Lorna and shone a torch into the dark opening. When he did that, Lorna wiggled out of the opening space, snatched the hard hat off Gideon's head and slung her rucksack back into the opening, to push ahead of her. "I'm not stupid, Gideon. If it looks bad, I won't go there."

"You're not the same as you used to be," he said, reaching up to turn on the safety light on top of her hat.

She smiled. "Is that a compliment?"

"Maybe. The Lorna I remember wouldn't have done this. She wouldn't have put on the hard hat and crawled anywhere on her belly." A soft smile curved across his lips. "I'm proud of you, Lorna," he whispered.

Words she would have loved hearing years ago. "It's mutual, Gideon. What you do…I'm proud of you, too." She looked deep into his eyes and what she saw there was the Gideon she'd first known—the one who'd existed before the weight of their individual worlds had come crashing in on them, the Gideon she would have stayed married to for ever. She blinked, trying to shake off the bitter-sweet spell coming over her. "So, tell me what to do."

He blinked, too, perhaps trying to rid himself of that same bitter-sweet feeling. "It's stable enough. I've had a good enough look to know it's not going to come down on you if you're careful inside. So, first, you're not going to get in too far. The middle of the structure has collapsed all the way down, but there's more clearance around the edges, which is where you need to keep to. Don't bump any of the boards along the way, and if anything shifts, get the hell out. Don't take *any* chances, Lorn."

"You almost sound like you care," she said, dropping to her hands and knees then crawling back to the opening. Once there, she slid on in on her belly.

"Maybe I almost do," he said under his breath.

"I heard that," Lorna called back. More than that, her heart felt it.

Inside, within seconds, Lorna's marginally lighted entrance turned into a dark chamber, illuminated only by the narrow beam coming off Gideon's hat. It was a cold, shadowy world in there, with the mud under her belly and her back mere inches from rubbing across what she assumed to be the school ceiling.

"Lorna," Gideon called from outside. "Anything? Can you see anything?"

Nothing that she wanted to see, like Tom sitting there waiting for someone to reach him. Or Dag, doing the same. "No, not yet," she yelled, as she shoved her medical sack in front of her and continued to squirm along on her belly like a worm. Every few feet she stopped and turned her head so the beam would cover the area, hoping to find…well, she wasn't sure what. A survivor, definitely. Or no one in there at all. "Tom," she called out. "Tom, can you hear me?"

No answer. So she moved on. Stopped some way down, repeated the process, then moved further in.

By the time she reached a little more open expanse, where she could push up to her knees, it seemed like she'd been crawling for ever. A quick punch on the light-up button on her watch revealed seven minutes in. And she was already exhausted, and sweating so hard she was having cold chills. "Tom, are you in here? Is anybody in here?"

She held her breath and listened for a second. Nothing…nothing…then suddenly a faint scratching. Was it Tom, or one of the children? Or only a rat moving into his new digs for the duration? "Hello," she called out. "Is there anybody in here?"

She waited, and again she heard a faint scratching. This time she pulled her torch from her rucksack and shone it back and forth.

But there was nothing to see, except more of the wreckage. Still, she couldn't shake the feeling that she wasn't the only one in there.

"Lorna!"

Gideon's voice was distant. She wanted to call out to him, but somehow, deep into this hollow cavern, that didn't feel right. Would a vibration from a loud voice rock more of the debris loose? Suddenly, she remembered the two-way radio, and fished in her pocket to find it. "Hello," she practically whispered. "Can anybody hear me?"

"Lorna?"

It was Gideon's voice again.

"Are you OK? Do you see anything?"

It was nice to hear his voice. After all these years, she'd never expected to think that. But right now there was no one in the world she trusted more than Gideon to get her through this. "Nothing," she replied. "I've still got some room to go forward, but not much. And I'm fine."

"Look, I've got more volunteers out now, looking for Tom. No sign of him anywhere out here."

Which meant he was, most likely, in there. As both she and Gideon had thought. "I'll keep looking," she said. Stuffing the two-way radio in her rucksack, Lorna pushed forward, half crawling, half sliding on her belly, until she could see a solid obstacle. She wasn't quite sure what it was. A wall, perhaps? Just a pile of debris? On impulse, she began to crawl in that direction and after a few feet two eyes glowed out of the dark at her. "Dag?" she ventured.

The dog whimpered, but made no attempt to get up.

"Good boy," she said, moving towards him. It was hard to tell what he was doing, but from his pose he looked to be lying over something…guarding it. "Tom? Is that you?"

In answer, Dag whimpered again. This time, a cold chill shot up Lorna's spine. Dag wasn't alone. "It's OK, boy. I'm on my way."

It took another few minutes before Lorna reached the dog, and when she did she found what she'd expected. Crawling up alongside Tom and pushing herself to her knees, Lorna's fingers immediately went to his pulse, but she retracted them in a split second, and raised them into the light from her hat.

Blood.

Grabbing her torch, she shone it down into the cold, lifeless face of Tom McCain. Dead from a crushed windpipe. Guarded faithfully by a rescue dog who understood the sad verdict.

And under Tom…"Hello," she said to Dag's other charge. At first, Lorna couldn't tell if the child was a boy or girl. But as she rolled Tom's body to the side and pulled the child over to her, she saw a muddy pink ribbon in her hair. Fingers to the little girl's pulse found a nice steady one. Respirations were even, no sign of bleeding or other trauma. She was awake, too frightened to speak, and blessedly alive. Injuries, if any, to be determined later, Lorna decided as she pulled a disposable thermal blanket from the rucksack and wrapped it around the child.

Then she clicked on the two-way radio. "Two survivors," she said. "Dag, and a child." She paused for a moment. This was the part she hated. Clicking back on, she drew in a deep breath. "I'm sorry, Gideon. Tom didn't make it."

What she heard on the other end was a gasp, then a choke.

What she saw in her mind was the look on Gideon's face.

CHAPTER SEVEN

"SHE'S doing fine," Gideon said, sitting down next to Lorna in the hospital tent. He was referring to the child Lorna had found in the school. Maria, they were calling her for now. "She's still a little shocky, but after what she's been through, she's doing amazingly well. No injuries except a few scrapes and bruises. Jason's taking care of her right now, and Priscilla's already taking pictures, getting them ready to send out to the local authorities in case someone from her family doesn't come around soon."

There was a sad mood hanging over base camp. No one was saying much, no one even mentioning Tom's name. But the looks on the faces…They were a close group, and the pain was pronounced. Yet they carried on. Each to his own job. Nothing stopped.

But everything had slowed down for a while. And there was a common bond in this sorrow between these people…one she didn't know, one she didn't feel. They grieved together while she grieved alone. She envied them that bond, that community of strength and feeling and care. They'd accepted her, and she'd even felt a part of them. But now she wasn't. It wasn't in anything they said or did, wasn't in a passing glance or even an avoidance. It was simply who they were and what they were, and who and what she was not.

"Tom had protected her with his body," Lorna said. Grasping a coffee-mug with both hands, Lorna tried to lift it to her lips but her hands were shaking too hard, so she lowered it to set it aside on the wooden crate next to the one on which she was sitting. But Gideon reached over and steadied the mug with his hands, allowing her to take a sip of the coffee. She needed the warmth to cut through the deep chill that wasn't going away, even though she'd been out of that collapsed structure almost an hour now. "Do they blame me?" she asked.

"For what?"

"For not saving him?"

"We don't blame, Lorna. Nobody blames anyone."

"They're all avoiding me. Even Priscilla. I'd thought…" Thought that maybe Priscilla had become a friend. "I've been pretty arrogant, haven't I? Just going out on the rescues, acting like I'm one of the team. That's been arrogant, and they resent that."

"No, Lorna. It's not you. We were the one who put you in the position to begin with. And what you're seeing now is a heart-break reaction…we've never lost anybody on a rescue before and we're just dealing with it the best way we can. They're turning to each other, to the people they know, and you're the outsider. It's natural at a time like this, and I think they're a little afraid you and your camera will intrude on their grief."

"But I wouldn't!" she choked.

"I know that," he whispered tenderly. "But they don't know you the way I do."

Brushing back a tear, she leaned her head against Gideon's shoulder. "I'm sorry," she said. "For so many things, I'm deeply sorry, Gideon." She felt almost as badly now as she had the day she'd lost their child. And for that, there had never been anything for which she'd been more sorry.

Except, perhaps, divorcing Gideon.

It was two hours later now, she was back to work, Gideon was still hovering over her, and her hands were still shaking a bit. Bless him, he'd become like a mother hen, hanging about in the tent with practically nothing to do, which wasn't at all like Gideon—being idle. He'd been there for her, though, and that's what counted, considering how bad he was feeling over Tom's death.

"How do you do this, Gideon? Time after time, how do you keep coming out to a rescue when you're called, knowing what you'll find, or what could happen?" she asked, as she prodded the belly of one of the victims brought in only five minutes ago. Old man, beautiful smile, frightened eyes. His vitals were stable, but she was doing a thorough physical on him anyway.

"I don't know how many times I've asked myself the same thing. To be honest, I've quit doing this a hundred times. Or more. I've convinced myself not to go out again, to go find a nice hospital and settle down to a steady surgical practice again. But then I get the phone call…and I see the faces. Maria, Ana Flavia…that child you pulled out of there who might otherwise not have been saved… That's how I can keep coming out. I remember the people we help, and that's what makes everything we go through worth it."

"Have you ever just walked away for a while? Taken time off? Had to go away just for an emotional break?" she asked, prompting the man to turn over on his side so she could have a look.

Gideon didn't answer for a minute. Rather, he concentrated on changing the bandage of the young man under his charge at the moment, gingerly pulling off the old one as it stuck to the man's head wound. "No," he finally answered. "I've thought about it, but something always gets in the way. And I think I'd probably be miserable after a couple of days. All this…it's more than what I do. It's who I am."

She knew that. To be honest, Gideon was more who he should be now than he had been when they'd been married. She wondered who he would have been had the marriage survived. In some peculiar way, perhaps the end of their marriage had been the beginning of the man Gideon was meant to be. It would have been such a loss if he hadn't made it to this place in his life. "How's Dani?" she whispered, as she helped situate her patient on his back again. There was nothing significantly wrong with the man…a few scrapes and bruises. But she wasn't going to turn him away. Not yet. Not until they needed the bed for someone more critical. "Any word from the hospital?"

"She's still in surgery," Gideon replied. "Her spleen was ruptured, so they removed it. Her pelvis was shattered in several places, and there was some substantial damage to her legs, so she's in orthopaedic repair right now. It's going to be a long recovery, and she'll have quite a go in rehabilitation once she's home, but her surgeon thinks she'll be fine."

Fine, but without the man she loved. Lorna ached so badly for Dani it was a physical pain. Telling her about Tom was going to be so difficult. Or maybe if she'd loved Tom deeply enough, something in her already knew he was gone. Had there ever been a time when *she'd* loved Gideon that much? Maybe. But so much of what they'd had together had been clouded by things that simply shouldn't have hurt them if they'd truly been together. Sadly, they hadn't been. If she'd seen that then…Hindsight really was so much better than foresight, wasn't it? "Who's going to tell her?" she asked.

"I will."

"Gideon, I'm so sorry about this. Is there something I can do to help?" She didn't know what else to say.

"So am I. And, no, there's nothing you can do." He placed a fresh bandage on his patient's wound, then turned to face her. "But I appreciate the offer," he said, his voice so sad it nearly broke Lorna's heart.

"It wasn't your fault," she said, fighting off the urge to walk over to him, take hold of his hand or do something to comfort him. But his arms were locked so tight across his chest now that the message was clear. He was shutting her out, too. Like everybody else there. She wasn't one of them.

"Blame it on the rain," he whispered, deliberately avoiding her gaze.

"Transport's here!" Frayne called from outside the hospital tent. "They're on a tight schedule so we need to get going."

Lorna nodded, then stood. "Is there anything else before I leave, or anything when I get back to the States? Call anyone? Make some kind of arrangements for you? Have more supplies sent down?"

"Don't break the news of Tom's death until I've had a chance to tell Dani."

She wanted to offer to stay, had thought about it for the past hour, but it was time to go. Her choice. Time to get back to her own world as Gideon's world didn't really want her. Besides, he hadn't asked her to stay. She'd thought he might, and she would have stayed if he had. But he hadn't, so she wouldn't. "You take care of yourself," she said, as she grabbed up her dufflebag. "I'll call you when I get the documentary put together."

"You take care of yourself, too." That's all he said, then he turned his attention to his next patient.

Just like that, it was over. Again. In a sense, another divorce. Only this time it hurt worse than it had before.

Lorna took one last look at Gideon before she followed Frayne to the truck.

"Are you sure about this?" Frayne called over the whoosh of the helicopter blades. He was inside, hanging out the door, shouting to her.

"I can't leave," Lorna shouted back. "Not yet." Deep down, she knew this was the right thing to do. The thing she had to do if, for no other reason, than they were short-staffed now.

"We're not going to get the documentary in on schedule," he warned.

"I've got a couple in the can." Meaning she had a couple documentaries already taped and ready to show. Back-ups, for an occasion such as this. A broadcasting necessity. "Tell them to use one of those."

"Any point asking when you'll be back?'

She shook her head.

Frayne cocked an inquisitive eyebrow. "Our bosses aren't going to be happy about this," he warned. "You know that, don't you?"

"Can't help it. I can't leave yet." She stepped back from the helicopter to wave him off. "Tell them I'm sorry to mess them up this way, but I'll have a great story for them when I get back." Standing ankle deep in the mud, the way she had when she'd arrived the day before, Lorna watched the helicopter lift off, and continued to watch until it was but a speck in the air. Once it was out of sight, she shifted her backpack from her left shoulder to her right, turned around, and started the long hike back to Gideon's camp.

Not too far ahead, a little man with bright brown eyes gestured her over to his donkey cart. He held out his hand for a few coins, smiling an absolutely irresistible crooked smile at her. "Why not?" she said, paying him then climbing into the straw in the back. His name, as it turned out, was Rubens, and his command of the English language was limited to very few broken words.

"Tourist?" he asked, as they made their way slowly back along the road. His accent was so thick it took Lorna a moment to figure out what he was saying.

"No," she finally said. "Doctor. *Doutor*."

Hearing that, he stopped the cart abruptly, pulling so hard on the reins that his donkey bucked up on his back feet and snorted his protest. Then Rubens turned to Lorna, who was still trying to find a comfortable spot in the straw, and started talking so fast she couldn't even pick out any familiar words. He was animated, loud, his face was turning red, and she took it to mean he either hated women doctors, or he had an emergency of some sort and, perhaps, needed a doctor. When he gave the reins a sharp jerk and his donkey did an about-face, she assumed it was the latter, and that she was being taken to tend someone in need.

Which turned out to be the case. Within ten minutes Rubens came to a stop in front of a tidy little frame cottage. It was gray, and splashed with mud, but standing strong, as were the other houses on this row. Outside, a pot of wilted flowers sat on the stoop, up under the roof overhang, and a tiny folding chair was propped against the wall, unopened. In the yard, a muddy dog greeted Rubens with a wagging tail as he climbed off the cart and helped Lorna out of the back.

He hadn't stopped talking to her from the moment he'd made the turn-around, and even on the way into the cottage he chattered away so fast that she wondered if anyone who spoke the language would even understand him.

The first room through which he escorted her was a parlor, with well-worn chairs and a floral sofa. The walls were lined with photos, dozens of them…children, old people, and all sorts of individuals in between. Family photos, she decided as Rubens hurried her on through the parlor, through the tiny kitchen and into a room at the rear. The door was partly shut, and the light off inside, but even before she had stepped in, she heard the rattled breathing of someone very sick.

"Andreza," he said, pointing to the woman in the bed.

Andreza looked to be near Rubens's age, probably his wife. "*Meu nome é Lorna e eu sou um doutor*," she said, glad for a fair pronunciation of one of her pat phrases, because, as she said the words, Andreza understood and raised her hand in thanks to take Lorna's.

What Lorna noticed immediately was the woman's blazing fever. Without a thermometer it was difficult to know just how high it was, but to the touch her skin was so hot Lorna instinctively knew she was in the extreme danger zone, perhaps four or five degrees above normal. And as if that hadn't been an obvious clue to her condition, her coloring certainly was. Andreza's normally deep bronze skin had taken on a yellowish hue, and a quick look into her eyes revealed to Lorna that the whites were also yellow. Jaundice. Meaning a compromised liver. "Has she been vomiting?" Lorna asked Rubens, as she mimed a gesture to indicate what she'd asked.

He nodded vigorously. Then he pointed to Andreza's head and back, indicating pain in those areas, too.

A viral infection, Lorna guessed, then raised her hands to gesture trembling. "Has she been doing this?" she asked, even though the man didn't understand the words. He understood the motions, though, because he nodded.

So, jaundice, fever, trembling, vomiting, headache and backache…backache meaning she could also have a compromised kidney. This wasn't looking good at all, and she desperately wished she had a better way to make a diagnosis.

Lorna drew in a pensive breath and let it out slowly, pondering the obvious options, finally settling on one. Yellow fever? It did happen here in South America and in sub-Saharan Africa. If that turned out to be the case, Andreza was most likely in the third stage already—past the early stage, which lasted three to four days, and past the remission that followed, which normally lasted about twenty-four hours. Usually, people were either cured in that short span or plunged into a life-threatening situation where that remission turned into a period of intoxication—multi-organ dysfunction, bleeding disorders, brain dysfunction, including delirium, seizures, coma…death.

She looked down at Andreza, whose eyes were shut. The poor woman had so many of the advanced symptoms, and there were so many questions to ask, so many answers she didn't have. And she didn't even have a thermometer!

She needed medical supplies, needed them fast. Unless she was totally reading the symptoms wrong, and she didn't think she was, Andreza was on the verge of dying. There wasn't a cure for the disease, but enough medical support could sustain her through the worst of it until the toxins were out of her system. That was if the damage wasn't severe enough to totally destroy one or more of her organs. And Lorna had no way of knowing how severe it was. "I want to get her to base camp," she said to Rubens, who had no idea what that meant. He simply nodded, and smiled.

"Can you carry Andreza to the donkey cart?" she asked, then did a simple pantomime to show him what she needed.

Rubens looked perplexed for a moment, then gave a slow nod.

"She's very sick," Lorna continued. "I have to take her to get help."

Even though he didn't understand the words, their seriousness did sink in, because he immediately went to a closet, pulled out two extra blankets, and wrapped them over his wife. Then he picked her up and carried her outside, laying her gently in the back of the cart. Within another minute Lorna was riding alongside her over the bumpy road, praying for a speedy trip and keeping her fingers crossed that the ominous rainclouds overhead would hold off until she had Andreza safely secured in the hospital at camp. If this was yellow fever, and she couldn't be sure without a blood test, Andreza's chances were only about fifty percent.

But at least she had a chance. Thank God she'd changed her mind at the helicopter. Thank God something she didn't yet understand had pulled her back to make things good with Gideon. Without that, Andreza would have died for sure.

Plodding along the trail with Max, two volunteers in front of him and two to the rear, Gideon went through the motions of searching, even though his mind wasn't on it. Tom…Dani…so many things to distract him. And Lorna…He already missed her. "You'd think I still loved her," he said to Max, who stayed at Gideon's side. "No offense, boy, but I was beginning to enjoy her company."

Max licked Gideon's hand, as if sensing his mood.

"I know, boy. I'm being too sloppy about this. Give me a little while and I'll be fine." Brave words, except he hadn't been fine the first time he and Lorna had split, and now, if anything, it felt as bad, maybe even worse than that first time. Back then, he had been almost glad to walk away. He still loved her, but the handwriting was all over the wall, and none of it predicted anything but problems. So getting out when he had had probably been for the best. Certainly they had both thrived since then. Become successful, found lives they loved, and moved on. But for him it hadn't been easy. Not emotionally, anyway. He'd missed her…for days, weeks, months…Maybe he never quite stopped missing her. Which was why he hadn't stop her from leaving. On a personal note, he couldn't go through all that again. Better to end it now before they went too far…or, at least, before *he* went too far.

Coming down the side of the hill, Gideon stopped and stared at the donkey cart making its way along the road. "Can't be…" he said, straining for a better look. Was that Lorna in the back of it?

He pulled out a pocket-sized pair of binoculars and took a look. "Damn," he muttered. She was hunched over someone…he couldn't tell who. Not good, he thought as he took off in a run down towards her. "Lorna!" he yelled, keeping an eye on Max, who was still on the ready for a rescue.

She rose up to her knees and waved to Gideon, but immediately dropped back down and went to the aid of her patient, who was in the throes of a seizure. "What is it?" he gasped, catching up with the cart.

Moving to turn the woman on her side as she convulsed,

Lorna looked up briefly at Gideon, who was running alongside. "Yellow fever's my best guess. Third stage. Classic symptoms. I want to see if we can get some prophylactic support going and sustain her through the crisis."

"Any others down with it?" he asked.

"Don't know. Rubens took me to Andreza, and she's the only one I've seen. But there could be. With all the rain and humidity…mosquitoes…" She shuddered. "There's a whole little untouched community over the hill and I wouldn't be surprised if there's more of this." She looked down at the woman. "Much more."

Gideon clicked on his radio. "Jason," he said. "We're bringing in a woman, possible yellow fever. There may be others."

"Don't have room, Gideon," he said. "Don't have the manpower."

Gideon ran an impatient hand through his hair. "Then make room. And contact the local authorities and see if we can find some hospital beds for them somewhere, because Lorna has a hunch that this victim isn't the only one." Smiling, he glanced over at Lorna. "And I trust her hunches."

"I'm pretty sure she has pneumonia, too," Lorna added.

"Probable pneumonia, too," he repeated to Jason, clicked off, then grabbed hold of the cart and hoisted himself into the back with Lorna, while Max continued to trot along at the side, perplexed at this disruption in the routine. "I thought you'd be gone by now," he said, pulling a stethoscope from the rucksack he carried.

"I thought so, too," she said, offering no explanation for her change of mind.

Gideon glanced at the sky as he put the stethoscope to his ears. "You won't get in trouble for this?" Then he took a listen to Andreza's chest, first the left side, then the right. Then back to the left. "Heart seems good enough, but both lungs are congested. Breath sounds completely diminished in her right lower lobe. Is she alert?"

"In and out. I think she's coherent, but it's hard to tell as I can't speak her language. Rubens was talking to her, though, and she seemed to understand. And no, I won't get in trouble."

He waited for a little more explanation from her, but none came. So finally, he asked. "Why?"

"Why, what?"

"Why did you come back?"

"Which version do you want to hear? The one where you were short-staffed and I felt guilty walking out? The one where I really felt good about the little bit of work I did here and simply wasn't ready to quit on it? Or the one where I wanted to make things right with us? We seem to be getting on well enough, but…I don't even know how to put it into words. I think there are some things left to be said. Take your pick. One reason, or all." She reached down and took hold of Andreza's wrist to take her pulse.

"For what it's worth, I'm glad you came back. And I choose all the reasons."

"How's she doing?" Gideon asked, bringing a fresh IV bag over to Lorna. She'd been huddled over Andreza's bedside for the past three hours, pushing medication, looking for signs of improvement.

Three solid hours of care now, and the most she could say was that her patient was resting comfortably. The antibiotics were kicking in because her fever had slightly decreased, and the oxygen was working because Andreza was breathing easier. But her urinary output was low, and too concentrated. And her eyes were still yellow. Not as bad as they could have been…she'd seen much worse. So that was a marginal point of optimism. "Holding on," Lorna said. "Which, all things considered, is about as much as we can expect right now."

It was already raining. Not hard yet, but the winds were

kicking up. Nothing serious predicted. The weather might even clear up later, according to the latest forecast.

"We'll get her transferred to a hospital as soon as we can get her out of here," Gideon reassured her. "Wish we could do it sooner, but we haven't found a bed for her yet."

"She stands a chance," Lorna said. "Until four hours ago, she didn't. Waiting a while longer isn't going to make a difference."

"Her husband feels bad. I was talking to him through one of the translators and he said that his wife kept telling him it was nothing. He said he could have gotten her help if he'd known, but they haven't seen an outbreak of yellow fever here for years. Poor guy is really torn up. They've been married twenty-five years, and he's really scared right now."

An outbreak...volunteers had brought in ten more victims in the last two hours. None were quite so advanced as Andreza, but the whole lot of them were sick. "The things people keep from each other," she said. Lorna checked Andreza's IV, then moved on to the next bed and did a routine exam of that patient, while Gideon did the same with another patient. "Sometimes it's just too frightening to admit," she said, as she took a quick temperature reading. "You know, or suspect, but saying it out loud makes it real. As long as you don't, it isn't real." That was the way their marriage had failed. They'd known, but they hadn't said anything out loud about it. Not until it had been too late.

"Look, Lorna. I'm going to see Dani later today if nothing serious comes in. She's doing pretty well, surgery was successful. Doctors are marginally optimistic about her recovery. But she..." He drew in a ragged breath. "She doesn't know. And it's only a matter of time until somebody tells her or she sees an account on television. So I've got to go."

It wasn't going to be an easy journey. Lorna recognized the stress written all over Gideon's face. He wasn't looking forward to this, and her heart went out to him. Telling Dani that Tom had died was going to be a terrible thing. "It's never easy," she said, instinctively reaching out and giving him an assuring squeeze on the arm.

"Come with me, Lorna."

"What?"

"To the hospital, to see Dani. Come with me."

"Are you sure?"

"Casualties aren't coming in right now, everyone we've kept is settled in and stabilized, and the next weather front won't set in until tomorrow, according to the forecast. We've got plenty of volunteers on clean-up, so it's a good time to leave for a few hours, and I don't want to take one of the rescuers out in case we do find more survivors. So I thought maybe you'd like to come."

It wasn't a journey she necessarily looked forward to, but Gideon was right. There was nothing critical going on at base camp right now. The yellow-fever victims coming in were easy care, the numbers of casualties were way down, and overall the entire operation was in a bit of a lull before the next storm. And maybe, away from all this, she might be able to have a talk with Gideon…one long overdue. One top of that, she might even get in a good interview. She still had her job to do after all. And interviewing Gideon away from the urgency of all this chaos might be a good way to go about it.

Except, two hours later, for the duration of the short helicopter ride to São Paulo, Gideon napped. Or at least he kept his eyes closed, pretending to sleep. Which was probably for the best as this little jaunt wasn't set to be a jolly one and he did need that time to collect himself for the awful task ahead.

The helicopter set down on a landing pad not too far from the hospital and from there Gideon and Lorna took a taxi to the Albert Einstein Hospital, a slow trip through crowded streets in a city of eighteen million inhabitants. It was an exciting mix of people—Hispanic, Asian, German, Balkan, Russian, Italian—all clinging to their own bits of heritage, which gave the city a wonderfully eclectic blend. There were museums and shops for everything imaginable. And the architecture was a fascinating jumble of old colonial and Spanish, along with a nice representation of ultra-contemporary. Vendors of every imaginable kind lined the streets selling fruit and produce, and shoes, and handbags and sun-glasses. And carved statuary sat on street corners overlooking the colorful bustle of everyday life. "Have you been here before?" she finally asked Gideon, as he'd not yet spoken.

"A couple of times. In and out. Haven't stayed. Normally, our rescues don't take us into the cities."

"Well, from the little I've seen of it, São Paulo is amazing."

"Third-largest city in the world. Me, though... I prefer my open space."

"That's right. You live in Texas now. Plenty of space there." Stiff, impersonal conversation, she thought. But she was drawing him out a little. And what did she expect anyway? Intimate details of the way he'd lived his past five years without her?

"It's convenient. Jason and Priscilla have a ranch there, and as he has the airplane...Doesn't matter where I live, anyway." He shrugged, drawing in a deep breath. Then he shook his head. "Do you know how much I don't want to do this, Lorn?" he whispered.

Yes, she did. And her heart ached for him. "Yeah, I think I do." Lorna glanced up at the green glass canopy covering the entrance as the taxi came to a stop. The hospital was large and modern. Very welcoming and warm in spite of the dreaded task ahead. To the casual observer it looked like the place in which you would want to be treated. To a physician, it looked like a valuable medical resource. Modern. Practical. Brimming with current technology. To Gideon, she was sure it was looking like a long dark tunnel through which he didn't want to walk. "She needs to hear it from you before it makes the news. And it will, Gideon. These things can't be stopped."

"Spoken like a true newswoman," he snapped, stepping out

onto the sidewalk then extending a hand to help Lorna out. "The story must go on, no matter what. To hell with everything and everyone else as long as you break the story."

She blinked her surprise over this total change in him. "That's not fair. I could have had that story on air hours ago. But I didn't. What I said was the truth, though. By now somebody else has it, and it's being processed, if not already broadcast. That's the way the world works these days, like it or not. Everything is just a breath away when it comes to technology. Bounce it off a satellite and send it anywhere in mere seconds, snap a picture of it on your phone and send it home. And, believe it or not, Gideon, I don't have a thing to do with all that so don't take it out on me!"

"Guilt by association," was all he said as he held open the hospital door for Lorna, and they went inside. Then, as they crossed the lobby, he did the oddest thing. He took hold of her hand.

She didn't flinch when he took hold. Neither did she pull away. Her hand in his…it was a fit she remembered, and one that, right now, was sending just the slightest chill up her back in spite of his dark mood. But she forgave him that, considering what he had to do. "Nice hospital," she said for a lack of anything better.

"Full service, five hundred doctors on staff. They even have an all-doctor orchestra."

"Maybe you could have a go playing your drums for them."

"You remember that?"

Did she ever. On the nights when he'd come home frustrated or keyed up from his day in surgery, he'd beat out his emotions on his drum set. She didn't know enough about music to tell if he was good at it, but he did have nice rhythms. "How could I forget it? You were the source of many good headaches."

"But you never complained."

"There was nothing to complain about. I rather liked hearing you beat on those things."

He stopped, then looked at her. "I thought you hated it."

"What I hated was that when you were banging on those things, you were leaving me alone. I think I would have liked practically anything if we could have been together."

"When I was drumming, would you have come into the room if I'd asked you?"

Lorna chuckled. "With earplugs in."

"We really do have a lot of swampy water under that bridge, don't we?"

"Different life, different people. Maybe we should have stayed out of bed more that first year we were together so we could have become friends."

"Sorry I snapped at you just now."

"I understand. I'd probably be snapping, too, if I was the one who had to break the news to Dani. As much as you hate doing this, you're a good friend to do it, Gideon."

"Could *we* be friends now, Lorna?" he asked, just as they stepped up to the reception area.

She didn't have time to answer, because the girl behind the desk immediately asked who they were there to see, then gave them directions when Gideon told her. After that, they were in the elevator, then hurrying down the hall to the nurses' desk, where Dr Aldo Evangelista, Dani's surgeon, was waiting to see them.

"She's stable," he said, in amazing English. "Spleen is out, fractures are repaired, and she's sleeping comfortably now. We have her sedated for the pain, but she's fully coherent when she's awake. Asking about her dog. Wanting to know when her young man will be in to see her."

"She doesn't know yet?"

Dr Evangelista shook his head. "I thought the news would be better coming from a friend."

"But she's stable enough for me to tell her?" Gideon asked.

"I don't think one is ever stable enough to hear what she's about to hear. But physically, she's strong enough."

"How long will she be here?" Lorna asked.

"A month before we can transfer her to a hospital in the States. Maybe a week less, if she progresses quickly."

Gideon nodded. "I understand," he said. "We'll make the arrangements when the time comes." He followed Dr. Evangelista into Dani's room while Lorna went to the waiting area. She could have gone, too, but somehow it felt like an intrusion. Right now Dani needed Gideon. Only Gideon. He would be strong for her, take care of her, help her through the crisis.

Pouring herself a cup of coffee from a pot in the waiting room, Lorna sat down on a chair by the window and stared outside. *Could we be friends now, Lorna?* Had that been a rhetorical question, or had he truly meant it?

Could she be his friend?

Could she be more?

She thought about it for a moment as she watched the people on the street below, and the answer to both questions came so quickly it shocked her.

And pleased her.

And scared her to death.

CHAPTER EIGHT

"How did she take it?" Lorna asked. She hadn't gone into the hospital room while Gideon had broken the difficult news to Dani. It wasn't her place to be there. She wasn't even sure that being in São Paulo with him was her place, but she was pleased he'd asked her to come along. And she did want to be there to support him.

"She's sedated. She heard the words, but I'm not sure the full impact of them sank in. At least, not right then. It's going to take her a while to fully understand it, I think. But her parents and sister are on their way here, which will be a comfort to her, and after she has the people she loves with her they'll help her come to terms with Tom's death. It's easier dealing with that kind of a tragedy when you're with the people you love."

"You did let her know that we have Dag, and he's fine?" she asked, latching onto his arm as they strolled down the street.

"I told her I'd keep him with me until she's ready to take him back. Look, we've still got a couple of hours before we have to go back to base camp. Do you want to have dinner with me? The *paulistanos* here have raised dining to an art form, so the world's the limit—Japanese, French, Italian, German, Portuguese, African—pick your cuisine."

They settled on Portuguese, and chose a nice little café three blocks from the hospital. It was brightly decorated in intense colors…reds, blues, greens, with parrots and flowers painted on the chairs and tables. Because in Brazil the main meal came at the middle of the day, they ordered light fare as it was early evening—*palmito*, a palm heart served in a salad, and *aipim frito*, deep-fried manioc root, with *quindim*, a richly sweet egg yolk and coconut custard, to follow. To relax before the meal arrived, they ordered *capirnha*—the favorite national drink, made from an unusually potent sugarcane rum called *cachaça*, crushed lime, sugar and water. It was a particularly refreshing drink, Lorna thought as she relaxed back into the banquette and took her first sip. Refreshing, but a bit surprising that she and Gideon had ordered exactly the same things. When had her taste in food become so much like Gideon's? She thought back to the time they'd been together and realized they'd always ordered the same things. It was amazing how those details had slipped away from her.

"So, besides your rescue work, what else do you do with your life?" she asked.

"I like to go out to schools and talk to children. They respond well to Max, and somewhere in the hour they allow me I usually tell a few fun stories and teach a few survival techniques. I've also started a program for kids, teaching them how to get an emergency pack ready—a three-day supply of everything they'll need during an emergency. The goal is to have them prepare one pack for every family member. We send them the empty backpack and a list of the things they'll need. Then when they've got it set up, they send us back a picture and we pop out an official *I will survive* T-shirt to them."

"That's amazing!" She'd had no idea he was so involved like that. "A brilliant idea!"

"Not so much amazing as it is important. Kids are resourceful and smart. Give them a little responsibility and they'll do a good job of it."

"How many of these backpacks have you had stuffed so far?"

"Over a thousand. But the program is young. We've only been doing it a year and we're hoping to double that number within the next six months."

"It's worthy, Gideon," she said. "I'm proud of you."

A slight smiled crossed his face, replaced by a faint blush. "What it is is a start. It'll get better."

He was so modest about this. Come to think of it, he'd always been modest. Another one of those details that had slipped away. But now she did remember that about him, how he'd never liked to talk about his accomplishments or successes. A truly modest man in a world where modesty was a fast-dying trait. She liked that. Sadly, though, she couldn't remember ever thinking about it before. It was one of those things she should have loved about him, but, she'd never given it much of a thought, just like she'd never given thought to their identical tastes in food. Her loss. And in so many ways those losses were beginning to add up. "Can I talk about it on air?" she asked. "Run a special feature on it, something apart from the rescue operation? Perhaps follow you to a school for one of your talks, then interview several children who have made their survival kits?"

"That's all it ever is with you, isn't it?" he snapped. "Take what you can so you can turn into a story for television. Do you ever get away from that?"

She blinked back her surprise over this sudden change in him. "We all do what we have to do, Gideon," she said, as the waiter placed the platter of *aipim frito* in the middle of the table. "And I'm so sorry you don't approve of the way I choose to be a doctor. But you never did, did you? From that very first day when I decided to take the television job, you hated it, and resented me for taking it. But guess what, Gideon? While what I do might not be seen as applaudable as what you do, I do serve my patients, and my audience, in my own way." She turned to the waiter. "I'd like to change my order to *salgadinhos*." A small pastry stuffed with meat and cheese, and something completely different from what Gideon had ordered just to prove that the two of them weren't alike. Not at all! Ordering the same things from a restaurant menu didn't make them that way, no matter how sentimental she was getting about it.

"All those times you ran off and left me alone while you were out on a search and rescue, I never complained. I supported you in your choices, but when I made a choice for myself, what did I get? Arguments. A demand to quit. Little barbs about how I was wasting my time. It was fine for you to do what made you happy, but in your opinion I wasn't entitled to do the same." So much venom coming out, but maybe it was time. "So yes, that is all it ever is with me. Because, like you, what I do is who I am. It used to bother me that you couldn't accept that…" She shook her head. It still did bother her. More than she'd realized. But instead of arguing any further, she reached for her *capirnha*, took a long drink of it and tried to relax to the nice mellow feeling it caused.

"I never told you about my parents, did I?" he said, his voice low, and stiff.

Actually, he hadn't. They'd died before she'd met Gideon, and whenever she'd asked about them he'd changed the subject. "Not much," she conceded.

"They were journalists. Both of them. Television journalists, like you. Except they were actually reporters, always being sent on assignments somewhere in the world. Wars, uprisings, riots, you name it and one—or both—of my parents were there."

She knew they'd been reporters, but not what kind.

"When I was young, I suppose I considered our life normal. But it wasn't. Neither of them were ever there. Oh, they came around, spent a few holidays, popped in for an occasional weekend. But for the most part I was left in the charge of a cousin or a grandparent or a kindly aunt. Anybody they could find to take care of me. And it wasn't easy, Lorna, because nobody wanted me, including my parents. In fact, they never failed to let me know that I was the result of a faulty diaphragm. Had my mother's birth control not failed, they would have lived a life free of the encumbrance I was to them. When you're a little boy who just wants to see his parents occasionally, knowing that hurts."

When you were an adult, it still hurt. She could see the pain on Gideon's face. "Why didn't you ever say anything?"

"What was there to say? That you were marrying someone whose parents didn't even want him?" He shook his head. "When they were killed in a plane crash on their way to do a story on a tribe, oddly enough here in Brazil, I didn't even go to the funeral, because had it been different, had I been the one killed, they wouldn't have taken the time to come to mine. A relationship like that really doesn't merit much discussion."

"Which is why you hated my going into television journalism," she stated. "Because you'd lived a miserable life already because that's what your parents had done."

"Consciously, I don't think I equated the two…"

"But subconsciously you couldn't separate them." She reached across the table for his hand and, for an instant, she felt a spark. It was only her imagination, of course. But it felt like the same spark she'd felt the first time he'd touched her. "I wish I'd known."

"Would you not have gone through with it?"

Good question. And she really didn't know the answer. "I may have anyway, but I would have done it differently, instead of just springing it on you like I did after I'd already signed the contract. I'm sorry I did it that way, Gideon. We should have talked about it first."

He grimaced. "Well, I should have said something, too. But I never thought you'd end up on television… You'd never indicated an interest, then out of the blue…"

"You wouldn't have married me if I shown an interest before, would you?"

"I loved you, Lorna. That's one thing I'll never deny. I did love you. But would I have married you…?"

This was interesting. Not hurtful, like it could have been. It had been such an emotionally tough day for Gideon all the way around and, instead of taking offense, she admired him for admitting something that was so deeply painful. "It doesn't matter," she whispered.

"But it does. Because you were right. I shouldn't have made demands when you took that job. Intellectual over emotional, I should have been able to work it out better. And now, intellectual over emotional, I shouldn't be taking it out on you because, believe it or not, I'm proud of what you do."

"Are you really?" she said, tears suddenly springing to her eyes.

"Have been for years. And I'm sorry I'm so moody tonight." He let out a strained laugh. "I have to keep it together for everyone on the team during the bad times, and sometimes it's just not easy. But they expect it of me…"

"And *need* it from you, Gideon," she said sympathetically. "So, bad moods allowed between friends."

"Well, friend. Like I said, I do approve of what you've done with your life. You're good at it."

"And I'm flattered you've noticed," she said, glad that his mood was changing.

"I've noticed everything you've done." He shook his head almost sadly. "Since the divorce, I've noticed so many things about you, Lorna."

Dinner was quiet, contemplative, introspective for both of them. Gideon ate his share of the manioc without saying much more to her than he already had, and he was working his way through her leftovers when his cellphone range.

He answered his call, mostly listened, then clicked off and stared across the table at her. "This probably isn't what you wanted to hear, but we're not going back tonight."

He was right. She didn't want to hear this. Even the little diversion of dinner caused her to feel guilty being away for so long. She wanted to check in on Ana Flavia and Andreza, and she'd promised to sit down and look at the photos of Priscilla and Jason's children. "Why not?"

"Helicopter's tied up on an emergency flight. By the time it becomes free, it'll be too late. The pilot will have had too many hours in the air. So we wait until morning."

"And there's no other way?"

"We could take a taxi, but most of them won't go out of the city. Especially with the rain coming in later tonight. And as far as I know, there's no other option."

Unbelievable! Stuck here with Gideon. "They can afford to have you away from the rescue that long?"

"Jason's got everything under control. Besides, the operation never hinges on one person. We won't allow that."

"Except that Dani's out, and Tom's…" Even the mention of Tom's name brought anguish to Gideon's face, so she stopped.

Gideon pushed back from the table, hailed the waiter, and ordered himself a second *capirnha*. "And there's not a damned thing I can do about it," he said, once the waiter had taken the order and scooted away. "Trust me, I'd much rather be back there—"

"Because anything would be better than being here with me," Lorna interrupted. "I've lived the life, Gideon. Remember? You don't have to make excuses. I've already heard them all."

"Didn't we have this argument before? A hundred times before?"

He was right. They had. "At least. But I guess there was one more in us, wasn't there?"

"Two wounded people, I suppose. I think we fought because it was easier than trying to figure out what was going wrong. We were good at it," she whispered. "Fighting was probably the thing we did best."

"Funny, I seem to recall that we did many other things better."

She looked over at him, a slight smile touching her lips. "Sex? Have a fight, go to bed. Those were some terrific moments, weren't they?" She cocked a wicked eyebrow. "Really terrific!"

He chuckled. "When it's good, it's good. Won't deny it. But I remember some other terrific moments, like all those evenings when you had to study and I had to catch up on reading my medical journals. You'd settle in at one end of the sofa while I'd settle into the other, and it didn't take more than a few minutes until we were snuggled into the middle, you still studying, me still reading. *Together.*"

"That was a fond memory for you?" That surprised her, because it had always been a fond memory for her, too.

"You always tried to spread out over more than your half of the sofa. It was subtle, but you'd wiggle your way in an inch at a time."

"Did not," she lied, even though that's exactly what she'd done. Not because she'd wanted all that space for herself, but because the more she'd wiggled in, the closer she had been to Gideon. She'd always liked being close to him, even when they hadn't been in bed.

"Then tell me why you'd always manage to persuade a foot rub out of me. You'd relinquish the space and I'd rub your feet in return."

"Because you have…*had*…magical hands."

"Magical hands that usually did much more than a foot rub," he said, leaning to the side a bit as the waiter put the *capirnha* on the table in front of him. The waiter tipped an uncomfortable smile in Lorna's direction, then backed away from the table.

"Apparently, he speaks English," she said, laughing.

Gideon reached across the table and this time *he* took hold of *her* hand. "There really were nice times between us, weren't there? I think we lost them in all that mess at the end, and I wish that we hadn't."

Nice times, nice foot rubs. They were so long ago, and so far away. It was time to remember them, she thought. Time to remember that she'd loved Gideon desperately once upon a time. And maybe it was also time to admit that she'd still loved him at the end of their marriage.

"One room, two beds is the best I could do close to the hospital, and across the street from where we're to be picked up in the morning," he said. Then Gideon quickly added, almost under his breath, "In my price range." It was a nice night. A little humid. A lot of energy exuded from the people milling around in the street. And while he should be feeling guilty over this little impromptu stay-over, he wasn't…wasn't even feeling guilty that he wasn't feeling guilty.

Strains of music were ringing from the shoulder-to-shoulder nightclubs packing the street—sambas and bossa novas and serenatas—and Lorna was actually dancing and mingling with the people, who were also dancing and mingling in the street. But all this was strange to him. Strange, and yet fascinating, because he could barely remember a time in his life when he'd enjoyed nightlife. Had he ever enjoyed it with Lorna? Probably not. From what he recalled of the year before they'd been married, they'd been too busy with their individual medical pursuits to do anything more than grab a pizza and a couple of beers at a local pub, and push it all down as quickly as possible. Then back to the usual grind in their separate directions. And in the two years they'd been married…well, pretty much the same thing. Everything had happened on the fly, with Lorna going one way and him going another.

Not much of a way to have a marriage. Thinking back on it, he was surprised they'd even stayed married that long. "And if you want a room to yourself, we'll have to stay in different hotels." He added that option, assuming she'd protest the original arrangement. Surprisingly, she didn't, and he was glad for that, even though he'd never admit it out loud, and would barely admit it to himself.

"Doesn't matter," she said, her attention more caught up in a beaded purse being offered to her by a street vendor. "Since we've already slept together."

Did that mean in the past, as in during their marriage, or in their brief encounters at base camp? He would have asked, but she was dancing around a vendor's cart now, laughing, bargaining in English with a man who didn't understand her language and waving to a clump of American tourists who recognized her from the morning news.

Amazing woman, he thought as he watched the way she literally drank life in. Amazing, adaptable, in love with life almost as much as life was in love with her. And he'd missed all that.

"Gideon," she shouted. "Do you need sunglasses? I think I've got us a brilliant bargain. Or a bandana? He has lovely bandanas, too."

"No," he shouted back over the noise of the people, who, like Lorna, were enjoying the night. "I'm fine. Don't need anything."

This little area was astonishingly lively tonight. People working up to the upcoming holidays—Christmas and New Year. Fireworks, boat parades, dancing, singing…they knew how to throw a first-rate festival here, and being here with Lorna during the heart of it might have been fun, because so far, even in this non-festival atmosphere, it had been fun watching her exuberance as she bought something from every vendor who stopped her, and a couple who hadn't. Beads, scarves, sandals, a stuffed doll, a straw hat she would never, ever wear…Her arms were loaded with bags, and he had almost as many as he could carry. Apparently, she wasn't done, because she was now taking two pairs of sunglasses and two bandanas from the vendor's cart and pointing to a string of plastic beads, ready to go into deep nego-tiation over them.

It was a magnificent night, and he was actually delighted to be part of it, if only in a vicarious sense. The colors, the sounds, the people…it really had been such a long time since he'd taken any time off, come to think of it. Normally, his days now were filled in much the same way as they had been when they'd been together…a quick pizza and a beer on the way to something else. Even though, technically, this shouldn't have been a night off, he was glad for the little diversion, glad to see a side of Lorna he'd never seen before. No wonder she'd become such a success on television. She was genuine. The smile she wore wasn't forced. When she waved to strangers, her greeting was sincere.

And when she worked as a doctor in his encampment, it was because she cared.

So in his opinions of her, maybe he'd been affected by their past. Or, more appropriately, blinded. Because pretty much every opinion, except the one in which she was fabulous, was wrong.

"Sorry about the room," Gideon shouted from the bathroom once he'd turned off the shower.

"I've stayed in worse," she shouted back, a slow smile coming to her face. "Remember Barstow?" An impromptu trip, the only one they'd ever taken. And what a disaster! Funny how, after a day that had turned out to be pleasant, the disaster was what had turned into an endearing memory.

"Hey, I take no responsibility for that mess! You were the one who wanted to stop."

Yes, she'd wanted to stop because she simply hadn't wanted to go back home so soon, hadn't wanted for their day together to be over. What she hadn't counted on had been that what had appeared to be a quaint little inn she'd chosen had been infested. Suffice it to say their stay-over had lasted all of three hours, and by the time they'd escaped to the car, they had both been a mass of itchy red welts. Of course, on the bright side, there had been some memorable moments after that as they'd applied salve to each other's wounds. Some *very* memorable moments. "It was a cute little inn," she defended.

"You have an odd sense of cute," he called back.

"You weren't exactly protesting when I asked to stop, as I recall." Thinking about the next two days they'd both had off from work as a result of their delicate condition was the best part of the memory, actually. Two whole days together. No place to go, no one to interrupt them.

Lorna shut off the light on the stand next to her bed, hoping that would also shut off those memories trying now to creep back in. Then she forced herself to think about her upcoming documentary and some of the editing notes she'd made earlier. And she was successful, putting together mental images of how she'd like the film to run, what kind of commentary she wanted to do as a voice-over. Successful, that was, until Gideon stepped out of the bathroom with nothing on but a towel wrapped around his middle. Then some mighty powerful memories came rushing back.

In the single light coming from the lamp next to his bed he looked so good, and she simply stared, unable to look away. As he wandered around to the slight gap between her bed and his without the slightest bit of self-consciousness, she struggled to avert her eyes when he turned his back to her. Even in the near-dark, though, she caught herself searching for the tattoo on his right shoulder—a modest one. A caduceus. Then there was the scar over his ribs on the lower left side. From a motorcycle accident…thirty-nine stitches. She remembered counting them after they'd been put in, and kissing each and every one of the tiny pinprick scars left behind after they'd come out.

As Gideon loosened his towel and it slid over his hips, Lorna still struggled to look away, tried to will herself to shut her eyes, to stare at the ceiling, to pull the sheet up over her face. Anything not to watch! But she was transfixed on the towel's painfully slow journey to the floor, and what was revealed to her in the dark shadows of the room when it was finally tumbled around his feet.

It wasn't like she hadn't seen and admired all this before, but now…

With a disgusted huff Lorna turned over on her side, her back to Gideon, and tried to dredge up her editorial notes once again. But for the life of her she couldn't remember a speck of what she'd planned for the documentary. Couldn't even remember the name of it, she was so distracted.

"No hot water," he said. "If you're going to take a shower, it's going to be cold."

Cold shower. Perfect! Just what she needed right now! Without a word to Gideon she jumped up and ran for the bathroom, planning for a good, long stay in the chilly spray, no matter how cold. But when he'd warned her that there was no hot water, he'd greatly understated that state. The water was positively glacial, almost a cascade of ice crystals on her hot skin. One minute into it and she was all goosebumps. So she hopped out, toweled off and put her clothes back on. None of that Gideon Merrill nonsense, sleeping in the nude like he was. Although there had been a time when she'd been glad that was his habit.

"That was fast," he commented, as she hurried over to her bed.

"I need a good night's sleep." She fought hard to keep her voice level, and hoped he wasn't hearing the high edge to it.

"Don't we all," he murmured.

After she crawled in and pulled the sheets up to her chin, she turned her back toward Gideon's side of the room and squeezed her eyes shut. Of course, the image there was Gideon. Pure Gideon. Naked. He was more muscular now. Leaner, and harder. She liked the years he'd put on. He looked a little older than his years, but it suited him. So did the slight creases around his eyes and the little flecks of gray she'd noticed in his hair. Subtle changes, yet good ones. Gideon was one of the lucky people who was growing better with age. She didn't want to think about him, but his presence was too close for her to think about anything else. Just listening to him breathe, hearing the rustle of his sheets, hearing the squeak of the bed as he shifted positions…

"You didn't get such a good bargain on the sunglasses, you know."

"What?"

"The sunglasses. You could have bought them cheaper from another vendor down the street."

So he'd been paying that much attention? That was a surprise, since she'd figured he'd probably been mildly put out by the whole shopping affair. "But he threw in the bandanas for free."

"You still could have done better."

"And the beads."

"Ah, yes. The deal-maker. Free beads. I could have got you free bandanas and twice as many free beads for the price you paid."

"Are you trying to start something, Gideon?" she asked lightly.

"I don't know," he responded, his voice rich and serious. "Do you want to?"

Suddenly, the moment she'd dreaded and wanted and desperately craved was so thick between them she could barely breathe. She'd fantasized about this almost from the first moment she'd known she was going to see Gideon again, so it may have been inevitable. She didn't know. But here it was and the decision was hers to make, the first move her choice. She wanted it, and nothing in her would be so silly as to deny what she wanted when she could, at last, have it. They were adults after all, they knew what they were doing. And they were so good at it. Yet she was unexpectedly nervous…almost as nervous as their first time together nearly eight years ago.

Of course, that had turned out to be a surprise—a nice one. A night that had spoiled her for anyone but Gideon.

Now, though…Lorna swallowed back the jittery lump in her throat. "Yes," she said. "I want to." And there was no hesitation or indecision. Because she did want this…want Gideon…in more ways than she'd ever counted on.

Without waiting for a further invitation, Gideon threw back his sheet then crossed over and climbed into Lorna's bed. When she turned over to look at him in the one dim light next to his bed, he was grinning over at her and arching his eyebrows and… She knew the look. Remembered it so well. Had always fallen for it. Was falling for it now.

"Gideon, are you sure…?" The air was suddenly electrified with what came next. It always came next, and she had no will to fight what she needed so badly from him. And only from Gideon. Always and only from Gideon.

"You're still dressed," he growled, pushing back the sheet.

"Then do something about it." She was already molding herself to the hard lines of his physique…lines that had always fit to her so well. Lines that fit her like nothing in her life ever had. Or ever would.

Positioning himself over her, Gideon lifted Lorna's hair and lowered his lips to the back of her neck, with a trail of tiny, sizzling kisses going from left to right. She gasped as he moved around to her most sensitive spot, and loved that he remembered how his kisses there had never failed to draw a shiver from her.

"I love it when you do that," he whispered.

"So do I, love it when you do that." She started to move to pull off her shirt, but he stopped her, and for a brief moment just held her pressed close to him. She tilted her head to lean against his shoulder and close her eyes. "I love everything you do," she whispered, burning with the heady sensation of wanting him. "Always have." *Always will.*

"Like this?" His fingers probed under her shirt, pressing into her tingling skin, causing her to moan aloud. A deep, sexy chuckle rumbled in his chest. "I suppose that answers my question, doesn't it?" he said, moving his hand to ease aside her lacy bra, then allowing his fingers to outline the circle of her breast.

The soft massage to her breasts sent streams of fiery desire flowing through her, and Lorna threw her head back and drew in a long, quivering breath. "Yes" she panted, sliding her hands down between them to stroke him into pleasure the way he pleasured her.

Before she had a chance to do anything more than find the object of her quest, Gideon pulled her up from the bed and with almost frantic hands pulled her shirt over her head and tossed it across the room. The bra came next.

"You were always good at that," she said, as her bra went flying over to his bed.

He bent to place a light kiss on her breast, then looked up at her, grinning. "Had lots of practice a long time ago."

"And practice makes perfect." As he slid his tongue over her nipple, and it pebbled for him, she drew in her breath and held it, savoring the sweet memories, savoring the moment. The touch of his tongue as it made a delicate circle caused her other nipple to pebble in anticipation, and Lorna shut her eyes to savor every last morsel of the sensation. "This is so bad," she gasped. "What we're doing, the two of us again…"

"Bad?"

"When bad is good, and good is so bad."

"Want to see what's really bad?" he growled as he pulled off her panties.

Thank heavens she'd put on something other than her sensible whites. Had she pulled out the hot pinks because she expected this, or hoped for it? A little subconscious nudge into Gideon's bed? "I love good," she purred. "Almost as much as bad."

He reared back and grinned at her again—a devilish, audacious grin that told her exactly what he was thinking. "And I love to be pleased." He arched his eyebrows. "By you, being bad. So please me, if you think you can."

"If I think I can? Since when weren't you pleased by what I did?" She stared boldly into his eyes as she slipped out from under him and pushed him down into the pillows. "As I recall, you were always very pleased." She rubbed her hands over his chest, starting at his throat and winding on down across his flat belly, stopping just above his erection. Then she climbed over him, straddling his middle. "And if you want to be pleased by me, you'll have to do some pleasing yourself." She rubbed her hands back up his chest as she nestled herself down over him. "Pleasing, Gideon?"

Lorna," he gasped, his voice so rough and roused it stirred her even more than she already was. It was such a turn-on, being able to do that to him, and with so little effort. And it was even more of a turn-on having him do that to her with even less effort…just one look. "Is it getting bad yet?" she asked, beginning to rock slowly atop him.

"So bad that if you don't stop…"

"Don't want to stop, Gideon."

Gideon groaned, sliding into her rhythm, matching hers to his. Faster and faster…

"Just one time, Gideon," she gasped, so close to the edge she couldn't pull back. "Do you understand that? Just this once."

"Understood," he also gasped. Then he slipped his hands up around her waist and held onto her as she arched to him while he drove his heat deep inside her.

Over and over, the friction, the rhythm of body meeting body…it built to the release that raked a scream from her lips and a moan from his. Then, even before she'd found normal breath, Lorna looked down at Gideon and smiled. "Well, maybe once more."

A perfect ending to the night, she thought as he pulled her down to his chest and merely held her there until he was as ready again as she was. More perfect than anything she could ever remember, including every other moment in bed with Gideon Merrill.

As Lorna leaned back into the pillows, so relaxed she could have melted through the sheets, she listened to Gideon's breathing even out, wondering how perfect could have gotten so much better, and trying not to pay attention to the obvious answer trying to wiggle its way into her thoughts.

CHAPTER NINE

ANOTHER gray day. They'd been hustled into the helicopter far earlier than she'd expected, and now they were back at base camp, life as normal, or at least as normal as it could be under the circumstances. Gideon was directing his rescue work, out with his volunteers on a different site that morning, and she was in the hospital, tending to the steady trickle of new patients coming in.

More rain had come while they'd been making love. More houses washed out, more people to pull out and take to safety. And she and Gideon had made love twice more during it all, like all the years separating them didn't exist.

Now, this morning, last night was practically reduced to an afterthought. On top of that, Gideon was moody again. Actually, he was barking worse than any of the rescue dogs could bark. And, yes, it did hurt a little. Not that she'd expected anything to come of what they'd done the night before. But, still, they'd gone from pleasant to this, and she simply didn't know what to think. It was all either up or down with them, and nothing in between. In the end, they were still a divorced couple who'd never really resolved anything between them. She understood more. And saw her failings in their marriage rather than fixing only on his. That was good. It was also necessary because, as difficult as it was to admit, she shared the blame. Maybe now that she was admitting it, she could truly move on.

There was another admission, though. It had fought its way in all night, and now, in the full light of day, it had its hold. She was in love with Gideon again. Maybe she always had been. Nothing between them had changed, except her feelings. Which wasn't good because now that she knew why he'd never wanted her to be a journalist, it was foolish to think that he'd changed. Admitting something out loud like he did didn't alter the facts. His life had been hell because of his parents' occupation, and deep down he transferred those feelings to her because she shared that similarity to the Merrills.

Sure, they could have an affair, fall in love, fool themselves into thinking that they could work it out this time. But the bottom line would be the same. The root of the problem hadn't changed. He would live his life resenting her job as a television journalist, and she would live hers always wanting more of Gideon than she could ever have.

So in the end it didn't matter that she loved him. They couldn't make a go of it. *Again*.

"Gideon's in a mood this morning," Priscilla commented in passing. She was serving breakfast to the patients while Brian was busy taking vital signs. "I guess he's taking it pretty hard about Dani. Couldn't have been easy, breaking the news to her, but I'm glad he was the one to do it. Something like that should never come from a stranger."

Lorna nodded absently as she took a bowl of something that resembled oatmeal from Priscilla and handed it to Ana Flavia, who was busy trying on the new scarf and sandals Lorna had bought for her in São Paulo. "It was difficult, but it's always better knowing, and he didn't want Dani hearing it from someone else."

"You didn't film it or anything?" Priscilla asked cautiously.

Still that wariness. She was still the outsider. With them. With Gideon. "No. I didn't even go in. It was private and I didn't belong."

Priscilla gave a little nod. "I didn't think you would, but a few of the team wondered, as Gideon asked you to go along."

Purely personal, she wanted to say. I went, we made love. But she didn't. "I wanted to catch up on some interview questions I haven't had time to ask him," she lied. To be honest, she didn't know why Gideon had asked her along. Thinking it had only been for sex was one thing, but that wasn't Gideon. He didn't use people that way—not even an ex-wife. Had he wanted her support through a rough time? Or time to put things right between them? "I've still got a little work to finish before I go back." She was arranging transport out that afternoon. It was for the best. All that muddy water under a very old bridge was getting too deep now that their relationship had taken yet another turn.

"So, did the doctors have a prognosis for Dani's recovery?" Priscilla asked.

Lorna blinked the image of Gideon away. "Not specifically on how long she'll be here. But her surgeon thinks she'll make a full recovery, and she'll probably be sent back to a rehab center closer to home in about a month."

"How's she taking the news about Tom?"

"I imagine it hurts in ways only Dani could understand."

"I can't even imagine," Priscilla said. "I've never lost anybody close to me."

"I have…" Lorna murmured. Losing someone you loved…yes, she could understand that. "I'm sorry," Priscilla whispered. "I didn't know."

"It was a long time ago. And he didn't die. He just…left my life."

"Divorce?"

"Five years now."

"Regrets?"

"About the divorce, no. We weren't suited to each other. About the marriage…a few. But I landed on my feet, and I'm happy. It was a good decision…the divorce, not the marriage. Sometimes I still wonder what possessed me to do that…the marriage, not the divorce. The follies of raging hormones, I suppose." Or just plain loving a man she shouldn't have loved. And that was far stronger than raging hormones.

Priscilla laughed, turning the tone of the conversation from downcast to much lighter, which came as a welcome relief to both women. "One of *those* relationships."

"One of those," Lorna said on a wistful sigh. It was so easy, talking to Priscilla. She hadn't really had much time for friends. All the hours she spent on her various jobs simply didn't permit it. But it was nice sitting here, chatting, and under different circumstances she could see herself becoming great friends with Priscilla. Of course, to do that meant involvement with Gideon, and once she left here Gideon would become part of her past. Again. "Came and went before either of us noticed. At the time, you look at divorce as the only way out. And you're relieved when it's over so you can get back to your own life." She looked over at Priscilla. "Except the one thing you don't realize when you're going through it is that your own life truly is part of his life. For better or worse, and all the bitter feelings aside, there are good moments, and sometimes it's so hard to adjust to the fact that you won't have those good moments again…that they're over. Out of your life."

"You loved him when you divorced." It was a statement, not a question.

"In a way, I suppose I did." He'd been the father of her child…their child. How could she not love him for that, even if their child had never been born?

"And you never thought about having another go at it? I mean, Jason and I have some terrible fights. Every couple does. But in the end we put whatever we were fighting about into its proper perspective, realize that what we have is far more good than it is bad, and have a good laugh over how silly we were to have the fight. So did you two ever…?"

"Actually, yes. We did get back together briefly. But it didn't work out. If anything, I think we realized just how far apart we truly are."

"That's too bad, Lorna. I like happy endings, and we're not getting enough of them around here lately. I'm sorry you didn't get yours…at least, with him."

Lorna shrugged. "So am I," she said, on a wistful sigh.

It was a damned waste to lie here in bed. He wasn't tired. If anything, he was eager for more work. But rules were rules, and this was his time out. If ever there was a time to lead by example, this was it—for the sake of the team. They were grieving, at a loss for what to do, what to say. And now that the work load was down, it was showing on them. Tempers were flaring a bit, his included. Even the always even-tempered Harry Lawson had picked a fight with the even more even-tempered Richard Eggington a little while ago, and Gwen Spencer had all but jumped down Brian Fontaine's throat. People were edgy, and it wasn't the time to argue with Jason about taking his mandatory two hours off. So here he was, itching to go back to work, with nothing but empty time ahead of him.

Empty time in which his thoughts were going to be filled with Lorna. Maybe that's the real reason he objected to this. He didn't want to think about her. Not after what they'd done.

"I really jumped into it this time," he said to Max, who immediately rolled over until he was cuddled up next to Gideon. "Knew what I was doing and I did it anyway." The dog sensed Gideon's mood, maybe even better than Gideon was sensing it right now. And as if to tell Gideon that everything would be fine, he nuzzled into him and let out a sigh to match Gideon's. Man and beast. There was a certain contentment there. But not enough to wipe out the mixed emotions surging through him. About Lorna. And Dani. Especially about Tom. "Damn it, Tom!" he whispered into the empty space. "Damn it to hell! Damn this whole bloody mess to hell!"

Sure, everybody going into a rescue knew there was always a chance they wouldn't come out of it alive. That was a given nobody ever dwelt on, though. Knowing that and seeing it happen were two entirely different things, and he didn't think he'd ever get rid of the image of Tom's body being carried out of the rubble. Even now, two days later, when he shut his eyes and saw it in his mind, Tom was smiling up at him from the stretcher, giving him the thumbs-up sign to indicate that he'd be OK.

It was an image that ripped at Gideon's gut and tore at his heart.

And Lorna…Dear God! After all these years, she was the one he wanted here with him right now, the one he'd wanted with him in São Paulo. That was part of the ache that had never quite gone away, he supposed. Something that had never been set right between them.

Then to go and do what they did… Not just making love, but doing it unprotected! No, it wasn't that he didn't trust her or anything like that. But…God, he didn't even want to think about it, about what had been on his mind all morning. It all went back to the miscarriage, the worst day of his life. One little slip with Lorna, although he'd wanted to slip, and suddenly all he could think about was when she'd been pregnant years ago, and how he'd let her down so badly when they'd lost the baby. It was something he couldn't take back, something for which he could never make up. Yes, he'd still been angry about her job. He hadn't wanted her on television, and over the months he had been away more and more, devoting more time to search and rescue rather than staying home and facing the real issues. His choice to go. It had been easier. But with the baby on the way…somehow that had made everything right. A fresh start for the two of them, with a little one on the way. But then that day never happened, and suddenly he'd become his parents—the ones who had always been gone when he'd needed them. He had gone in Lorna's worst hour, when she'd needed him most.

After making love to her last night, then realizing afterwards they hadn't been careful, that's all he'd thought about. She'd assured him it wasn't her time of the month to conceive, but that hadn't stopped the thoughts. And the guilt.

Even more, he was so distracted he couldn't think straight. So maybe it was time to send her back. Tell her they were winding down the operation and that he was anxious for the documentary to air. Out of sight, out of mind.

But never out of his heart. Which was why, since Lorna, no one else had ever truly been in.

Gideon's tent was zipped, but one of the volunteers had said he was alone in there, so Lorna unzipped it and tossed in her backpack. Then she crawled in after it.

He was alone all right. Just Gideon. With Max, of course. Gideon was turned on his side, his face to the tent wall. Max was curled up at his back, his head resting on Gideon's hip. Max was snoring, Gideon was not. And from the sound of his breathing, she knew he wasn't asleep.

"Jason kicked me out of the hospital for a couple of hours," she said, crawling over to the second bed. "For once, I didn't argue."

He didn't say a word. Didn't so much as change the pattern of his breathing. But Max pricked his ears and let out a friendly whine.

"So, what's this about, Gideon? This cold shoulder you're giving me?"

"It's time for you to go," he said, his voice unusually flat. "I have a couple of volunteers who will be here later today, and as this rescue is beginning to turn down now, we don't need as much manpower."

"Just like that, you're sending me away?" Actually, she'd come to tell him she was leaving, but having him do the deed hurt.

"It's my operation, my decision." He rolled over and propped himself up on his elbow. "I need your documentary to air more than I need you here helping. It's as simple as that."

"You can't always control everything and everyone in your life, Gideon."

"That's obvious. If I could, Tom wouldn't be dead. He'd have followed the rules and been alive to complain about it."

"Tom didn't do anything you wouldn't have done."

"He knew better."

"We all know better. And yet we do things we shouldn't, things that defy the odds. Brave things, like Tom did. And you know what, Gideon? No matter how you play and replay this tragedy in your mind, the bottom line will always be that Tom saved that child's life. He could have waited outside until help arrived, but none of the people who work in your operation would do that, and you know it. Not one of them would have stood by, listening to that child cry." She paused, and took a breath. "Tom's dead. You're blaming yourself, feeling that somehow you were responsible. But you weren't."

"You don't know me any more, Lorna. You don't know how I'm feeling about anything."

"Three years together gives me an idea. You've changed, but not that much." She settled down on the bedding and stared up at the top of the tent. It was daylight, too much sun coming through to sleep, even though she was exhausted. And her nerves were raw, another reason why she wasn't shutting her eyes. There were so many things pent up in her…emotions left over from their night together, concern for Gideon, an overwhelming sadness for all of Tom's friends. And especially for Dani. Lorna knew what it was like to lose someone you loved…her situation was different, but the love no less. For her child, for Gideon—what she'd felt over the loss of both in such a short time was something she still couldn't put into words. "For what it's worth, I've already made arrangements to leave. Don't know when. Later today, maybe early tomorrow. Either way, I'll be out of here soon, and you won't have to worry about fighting with me any more."

"For once we finally agree on something." He didn't say anything after that, In fact, he was uncharacteristically quiet, and as Lorna settled in, she listened to a breathing pattern that definitely was not one of sleep. Listened for the full two hours.

Another day, one just like the one before, and Lorna was listening to the rain beating down on the dining tent, each drop punctuating her dreary mood. Her exit had been postponed due to the weather so she'd kept herself busy in the hospital. It was practically empty now. No new casualties had come in for twenty-four hours, and the few that hadn't gone home or been sent on to a local hospital were lingering more from a lack of someplace else to go than the need for medical care.

She was sipping that awful coffee again, actually so used to it now that it didn't taste that bad to her. Her story was coming together, as much as she could put it together here in the jungle. She'd interviewed most of the people in Gideon's group, talked to a few patients who'd agreed to be seen on camera, prepared text for her voice-overs. There was nothing left. She'd talked to Frayne a couple of times since he'd left, and he'd said the film had gone together brilliantly. So basically she was more needed back in New York than she was here. It was time to do the job she'd come to do, to tell the story of the valiant people like Tom, relate the tragedies and show the hope and optimism in spite of the adversity.

"I'm leaving on the next transport out," she told Jason, on her way back to the hospital tent. "Might be in a couple of hours if the weather holds."

He gave her a curious look. "Have you told Gideon?"

"We talked about it. He agrees. I just wanted to let you know that when I get back to New York and get this piece put together, I'll give you a call so we can make arrangements for you to take a look. It'll probably take me about a week, as I've got some other things to catch up on."

"Hate to see you go, Lorna. You've been a big help to us, and I wish there was a way to persuade you to stay. Or join up as a volunteer."

It was nice he'd said that, but she truly wished it was Gideon expressing those sentiments. "I hate to go, too, but it's time. I've enjoyed helping, even though it doesn't feel like I've done that much. But as far as being recruited…it wouldn't work out. If I thought it would…" Well, that's as far as she thought because she couldn't thread in and out of Gideon's life. Too many difficult emotions in that scenario. And too many distractions for Gideon. He didn't need that.

Jason gave her an affectionate squeeze on the arm. "You'll keep in touch, won't you? Priscilla's really grown fond of you, and we'd like you to come down to the ranch to meet our children some time. Maybe after the holidays. Pick out the snowiest New York day in the dead of winter and come to Texas."

Down to the ranch was awfully close to Gideon. But she did value Jason and especially Priscilla as friends. Besides, Texas was huge. Surely, in all that open space she would be able to avoid Gideon. "I'd like that."

"You're not just saying that to be polite?" he asked.

"Not just saying that to be polite," she confirmed. "I'll come visit after the holidays."

Gideon and Max stood quietly behind a pile of rubble, looking down at the camp, at the hospital tent. "I hate goodbyes," he said to Max. "They just make an already bad situation worse." Maybe he should have been friendlier to Lorna after the night they'd spent together. Offered some hope that they could be more than a typical divorced couple, or told her how he really felt. But, damn it, he couldn't. He'd been through this once before, watching her leave him. Didn't want to do it again, because when it got right down to it, there was no way it could work out other than the way it had before—he going his way, she going hers. This time maybe the feelings wouldn't be so harsh, and this time they did have a better understanding of each other, something that would have helped them the first time. All that aside, it couldn't be anything other than what it was. Wishing and hoping just distracted him from the things he needed to be concentrating on.

Gideon scratched his dog behind the ears as he headed out to the south face of the mountain for no particular reason. He wasn't on the schedule to search, but he didn't want to be around Lorna because that would complicate his wobbly resolve. "So it ends, Max," he said, turning his back on the road, taking little comfort in the fact that he was doing the right thing. Besides, all the personal feelings aside, she wasn't experienced at rescue, and with her heart, she would put herself in the way of danger first and think about it afterwards. Like she had with Tom. So, getting her away from here was for her own good. Gideon mulled that over for a minute and decided to stick with that reason. It seemed so much better than wanting her out of there because he was in love with her and didn't know how to work it out.

Max gave him a speculative look, and Gideon laughed. "OK, I'm pathetic. Really pathetic. I let her leave me once…" And he'd regretted it pretty much every day since then.

Clicking on the radio, Gideon raised Jason. "OK, before you argue with me, I'm going up beyond where we pulled Dani out and have a look around. We haven't been over the ridge yet, and Max and I are up for it. And, no, I don't have anyone with me."

"Then I'll send someone," Jason said. "And no argument from you."

He wasn't in the mood to be bothered with other people right now, but he wasn't going to argue the point. "I'm going on ahead. They can catch up." He clicked off before Jason could respond, and tucked the radio in his pocket. Then headed up, his mind on Lorna.

CHAPTER TEN

LORNA was ten hours into her shift now and still waiting for word about her ride out. She'd thought she'd been leaving an hour ago, but the rain had started again, a whole new section of village was in jeopardy of collapsing, and the transport truck was in reserve to take patients out to the hospital in Francisco do Monte.

Right now, the rescue teams were out helping the residents evacuate, while minor casualties were beginning to trickle in. And her feet hurt. So did her back. But it still felt good to be doing hard work. The longer she was there the more she realized how much she missed that in her life. Once she got home she was going to make a change. She wasn't sure what, or how, but the result would be more time for real patient care. She was excited about that. Maybe Gideon would be excited for her, once she decided to tell him. She hoped so. She also hoped that now she understood better why he'd always resented her television work, that rift between them would be patched up a bit. It wasn't his fault he had felt that way, and now that she knew she could deal with it.

It was good he'd finally told her. Too bad he hadn't done that years ago. But perhaps he hadn't even thought that deeply about it then. Perhaps his reaction had come straight from the gut and hadn't made much more sense to him at the time than it had to her.

"You look dead on your feet," Priscilla commented in passing.

She was preparing to be off on the rescue with the others, but she stopped briefly to give Lorna a glass of fresh fruit juice. "Gideon wouldn't approve. You're over your time limit and right now he's being a stickler for the rules."

Lorna took a sip of the banana and coconut mixture and enjoyed the pure taste of it sliding down her throat. It felt good in her belly, too. Not like all that acidic coffee she'd been drinking so much of to the point she'd thought infusing it through IV would have been easier. "Gideon gave up his right to approve or disapprove of anything I do years ago when I divorced him," she said, amazed by how casually the words rolled off her lips.

Priscilla opened her mouth to respond, but nothing came out.

"Shocked?" Lorna laughed. "It was just as much a shock to me that I ended up here with him after all this time. Probably even more of a shock to him. But life has a way of playing these surprising little tricks on you."

"I had no idea. I mean, Gideon never mentioned…"

"He wouldn't," Lorna said. "It was rough on him…on both of us. A lot of difficult feelings. Sometimes it's better not to dwell on it, which, I'm assuming, is what Gideon has done."

"So earlier, when you said that you and your ex had gotten back together…" Her eyes blinked wide in surprise. "You and Gideon? Since you've been here?"

Lorna merely nodded, and not even demurely.

"Well, I didn't think there was anything left that could shock me, but I was wrong because you just did."

"The marriage was over a long time ago. We weren't ready for it…neither of us were." A difficult admission, but one that was so true. They'd been two people who had been so right for each other at such a wrong time in their lives.

"No wonder he was so grumpy when Jason told him you were on your way." She laughed. "Normally, Gideon's easygoing about everything and Jason and I both thought he was protesting too much. Which makes sense, now that I know the reason why."

"Well, he couldn't have been as grumpy as I was when I found out he was here. I think I wanted to face him, but I wasn't ready. Five years and you'd think I could have handled it better, but the thought of seeing Gideon again scared me to death,"

"And?"

"And, what?" Lorna asked.

"How was it, seeing him again after so long?"

"Gideon's an amazing man. Always was. I think seeing him again has made me realize just how much."

"Oh, that sounds like a bit of a hedge," Priscilla said, smiling. "The answer a well-practiced journalist would give. I think you saw him and all the old feelings just came pouring out again, and not necessarily the bad feelings. Or, am I getting too personal here? Just tell me if I am and I'll shut up."

"Not too personal. But I'm not sure I want to or even can talk about my feelings because, to be honest, I'm not sure what they are." She was the very definition of mixed emotions. "I walked out on him and never went back. My divorce, not his. My decision. And at the time I thought I had very sound reasons." Lorna tilted the glass of juice to her mouth again and took a sip. "Now I'm not sure."

"Well, this sounds like a talk you should be having with Gideon, so I'm not going to do any more prying." Priscilla reached out and gave Lorna's hand a squeeze. "I hope we can be friends in spite of your past with Gideon. Or the way it turns out with him now."

"I'd like that, especially since I already accepted Jason's in-vitation to come to your ranch."

"And I'm going to hold you to it. Look, I've got to get going. We'll catch up later, and if you want to talk…"At that moment Priscilla's radio clicked on and she was summoned to join the team. She scurried out of the tent and went to uncrate her dog, while Lorna watched the group assembling in the clearing. Gideon was going out for his second time that day, taking charge, calling out the orders, arranging the various smaller groups that would go on the hunt with him. This was so vitally his element that it made her heart swell just a bit. Yes, she was in love with him again…maybe it had never quit the first time. Whatever the case, in spite of the difficulties, just to look at him caused such an emotional stirring. And this time it was so different than anything she'd felt the first time she'd laid eyes on him. Better, fuller, more completing.

She thought back to the first time she'd seen him. It had been in passing. Gideon had been on his way into surgery and she had been running in the opposite direction to a Code Blue. They'd literally collided in the hall, and when she'd looked up to see the great, immovable force that had nearly knocked her down, she'd known she was looking into the eyes of the man she would marry. "The man I would love for ever," she whispered.

Part of that came true…he had been the man she would marry. But the man she would love for ever? Somewhere, deep down, she wondered if that part of the prophecy was true, too. And she was just now coming to realize how true it was.

Lorna turned away from the door and forced herself to concentrate on her patients—eleven minor casualties and a few leftover yellow-fever victims, all well on the mend.

And one very melancholy doctor with the potential diagnosis of a breaking heart.

"They just called in. They've got another twelve injuries on the way down. Gideon's on a rescue now, and he's not going to be back before the storm hits." Gwen was busy setting up for the next influx of patients, instructing Belinda Jennings and Ryan Hampton, the new paramedics who had just come in to replace

Tom and Dani, on how they were going to get everything ready. "Everybody else has been called back in. That's standard protocol during a storm. We don't let anybody stay out."

As Gwen spoke the words, a great burst of wind nearly ripped the hospital tent from its stakes. From inside the tent, Lorna looked up at the sky, frowning. Day after day of this, with more predicted. Well, so much for going home that day. Nature just wasn't congenial enough to let her to travel yet. "Is he going to be OK out there by himself?"

"Gideon's got Max. He's always careful. They'll be fine," Gwen said, even though the crease of hesitation that crossed her face didn't say the same thing. "And in case you haven't noticed, Gideon makes the rules but he doesn't necessarily follow them."

Gwen was a no-nonsense type. She was a large woman, with short curly brown hair and eyes that never melted into a soft smile, except when she talked about Gideon, then she took on the countenance of a caring mother as she was a good twenty years older than anybody else on the team. It was amazing, Lorna thought, all the types who came together for this. So many lives put on hold while someone went out to do a valiant thing. Someone, like Gideon. "Will anybody go out there to be with him? To help him?"

Gwen shrugged. "Don't know if he'll allow it. He's gotten pretty strict about the rules since the accident. He wants everybody in during the worst of the storm. Jason backs him up in that, and I don't think anybody's going to go against it. We've all been around for a while. Know what can happen."

Sadness passed over her face and Lorna knew Gwen was thinking about Tom. He had ignored the rules, split from Dani and gone in on his own, then paid the dearest price. Yes, they all knew what could happen. To any of them. "Well, I've been on duty too many hours now, so I'm going off for a while."

"And Gideon didn't say something about it?"

"Not a word." She smiled. "But he didn't know." As far as Gideon knew, she was long gone.

Lorna ducked out the door, straight into the rain. Instead of heading over to the dining tent for a bite of food, though, or to the volunteer tents to find an open bed, she dashed over to the central tent where the equipment was stashed and took a look at the latest rescue grid. Every rescue was marked, every site being explored located with bright red pushpins. No exceptions, not even for Gideon, and according to the chart he was back on the south face, going a little further around the wash than Tom and Dani had gone. He was there alone, though, as she could see his team on their way back in right now.

A queasy feeling landed in the pit of her stomach. One she couldn't explain, but one that scared her for no reason she could even begin to understand. Thinking about Tom…good intentions, the worst outcome. No, Gideon shouldn't be out there alone. Not in this. Not under any circumstances.

"Don't even think about it," Jason warned, stepping up behind her.

"About what?"

"About going out there with him. Priscilla told me about you two. I knew he'd had a relationship go bad in the past, had no idea it was with you. And she also said there are a whole lot of unresolved emotions going on. "

"He shouldn't be out there alone, Jason. You know that!"

"Sure, I know that, and that's exactly what I tell him every time he breaks his own rules. But it's Gideon's call, Lorna. He's smart. He won't put himself in the way of anything dangerous."

"Unless someone needs him," she said.

"Unless someone needs him," Jason repeated. "Gideon and I may be in charge of the teams, but when it comes to what Gideon wants to do…"

"No one's in charge of Gideon," she said. "And he listens to no one. Believe me, I know that."

"He'll be fine." He forced a brave smile, but the worry behind it shone through. "I'll send a team out as soon as the worst of the storm is over. Until then I'm not putting anybody at risk. I don't want to sound harsh, but we've already had one fatality from someone who didn't follow protocol, and I'm not going to do something I know isn't right just to force Gideon to do something he doesn't want to do. Like I said, he'll be fine."

She nodded, not at all convinced by Jason's words.

Jason must have seen the uncertainty because he pulled a radio out of his pocket and handed it to her. "Look, call him." Then he exited the supply tent to greet six volunteers carrying in three stretchers.

"Gideon?" Lorna said as she clicked on.

No answer. Just static.

"Gideon, come in."

Again, static.

"Gideon, it's Lorna. Can you hear me?" Now she was getting concerned. Jason hadn't been up that way, he didn't know how bad it was. And with two more hard rains since she'd last been up there…"Gideon, answer me! If you can hear me, answer me!"

But he didn't. And that's when she went to find Jason to tell him that Gideon might be in trouble. Problem was, every single volunteer and rescuer in the outfit was busy settling in the influx of new patients and doing the initial round of medical assessments, and there was no one free to go out looking for Gideon.

Except her! Damn the rules.

"Look, Gideon," she said to herself as she grabbed a rucksack full of medical supplies. "I'm coming out there, and you'd better be in trouble. Because if you're not…" She prayed that he was not as she slipped out of base camp and headed south, straight into the wind and the rain.

* * *

"Good boy," Gideon said, sliding his way up to one of the houses still standing on this side of the hill. Max knew someone was in there. Judging from Max's reactions, someone alive!

That was a relief.

It was also a relief that he'd sent everybody back, because from the looks of the ground up there, it was none too stable. In fact, he wished now he'd sent Max back, too. Since it was still raining, there was every chance the mud could turn into a river and wash everything on this path down with it. Which meant it was time to get the people inside that house out, and get the hell out of there himself. No heroes here, he thought as he fought his way up, each and every one of his steps sinking him ankle-deep in the mud.

It took another five minutes of slipping and sliding, falling down into the mud then pulling himself back up, before he finally reached the house. It was a bright orange, with cute white flower-boxes under the windows. Except the boxes held no flowers…only mud. And the front window was broken, leaving the muddy white curtains inside exposed to the weather. "Hello!" he called. "Anybody in here?"

"Hello!" a tiny voice called back.

A child! "Good job," he said, patting Max on the head.

Within a few seconds a small boy with a thick head of black curly hair appeared at the front door, trying to hide behind it as he opened it to Gideon.

"Meu nome é Gideon e eu sou um doutor," he said.

"Me nome é Zé Azevedo," the boy said tentatively.

"Well, Zé, I'm afraid that's where my knowledge of your language ends." He motioned Max over to the door, and immediately a broad smile broke out on the boy's face. Always worked with children. Bring in Max and everything was fine.

"Max," Gideon said, pointing to the dog as he tried to look past Zé into the house. It was dark inside, and from his vantage point he could see no one else. But the child couldn't have been more than five or six and, as close and protective as Brazilian families were, his parents wouldn't have left him here alone. So there had to be someone else in there. "*Mãe? Pai?*" Mother? Father?

Zé gave Gideon a curious look, as if trying to figure out his accent.

"Mãe?" he said again, wondering now if he was using the right word.

"*Onde está sue mãe?*" Lorna said, stepping up behind Gideon. "Roughly translated, I just asked him where his mother is."

"You followed me?"

"More like came to rescue you."

"Except I don't need rescuing."

"Well, it seems you do, at least in the sense of needing a translator." She glanced down at Zé again, and repeated, "*Onde está sue mãe?*"

"*Minha mãe é doente.*"

"She's sick," Lorna said, stepping into the house ahead of Gideon.

He came through the door right behind her, and his immediate impression of the house was that it was clean and tidy, except for the area at the front window where mud and other loose debris had filtered in. There were bright pictures on the wall...family members, he guessed. And a hand-made blanket covering the back of a rocking chair. Typical Brazilian flowery brightness with a blend of primary colors.

"In the back," he said, pointing to the closed door at the end of the short hall directly in front of them. Immediately, he threw off his rain slicker and brushed back his wet hair. "We've got to get them out of here because if this hill slides, the house won't stand." As attractive as the house was, there wasn't sufficient structure to hold it up, and every minute spent there put them all in greater risk. "You take Zé and head on back to base camp," he instructed. "I'll take care of his mother."

"Not before I have a look at her," she said.

"Lorna," he muttered, "this isn't the time to argue."

"Not arguing," she said, on her way to the back room. "Just telling you what I'm going to do." She opened the door to the back room, took one step inside, and sucked in a sharp breath. "Gideon," she whispered, "we have a problem."

Immediately, he stepped in behind her. "Damn," he muttered, clicking the radio on. Priscilla answered through a spray of static.

"We have a woman here, fully in labor. House is in jeopardy, and we can't take her out. I need as many volunteers up here as I can have… Tell them to come prepared to brace the structure, or dig us out if it collapses before we can get out. I'll also need whatever supplies we have to get this baby back down to base camp safely." He didn't know if the message was getting through. He could only hope

"Two," Lorna said.

"What?" he sputtered, clicking off the radio.

"Two babies. She's holding up two fingers, and I'm assuming that means twins."

"Great. This means we could be having a premature birth. Damn, that's not what we needed!" He clicked back on the radio. "I need more medical help, too. We've got twins coming…"

"Moderate contractions," Lorna said, laying her hands on Jussara Azevedo's round belly. She was already timing them, while Gideon methodically explained the location of the house to Priscilla, then repeated it in case it didn't get through the first time.

"I don't suppose you understand enough to know how far along she is?" he asked Lorna, after he clicked off the radio.

"Wish I did. But I don't even have my translation book along." She pulled back the sheet and exposed the woman's belly as Zé explained to his mother that Gideon was a doctor.

Jussara looked relieved for a moment, then she was gripped by another contraction.

"Don't need a translator for that," Gideon said, pulling the stethoscope out of his rucksack. He put the earpieces in and took a listen. "Her heart's fine, can't hear a damn thing from the babies."

Lorna smiled. "But I can feel them, and they're ready to get out."

"So, are you going to do the exam? She'll be more comfortable with a woman, I think." It wasn't the impending childbirth that made him uncomfortable so much as having Lorna there, during it. They had never talked about her miscarriage since the day it had happened, and even then the words between them had been so few. And so bitter. This had to bring back awful memories for her, because it did for him. Trying to get to the hospital to be with her, getting stranded at the airport, caught up in traffic on the highway...too late when he finally did arrive. Even now, thinking about the way he hadn't been there for her made him sick to his stomach. Sometimes he could still see Lorna's face when he'd arrived at the hospital that day...the pain, the anger, the fear. It always made him break out in a cold sweat, just like he was doing right now. Any other emergency, but not this...

He turned his back as Lorna did the preliminary exam. "She looks to be right at six centimeters," she said. "One hundred per cent effaced."

"So it could be a while," he said, still staring at the wall.

"Or right away. You never know with twins."

"Gideon," Priscilla called over the radio.

"Here," he said into his.

"We can't get...whole area...sliding...not safe." Static broke up the rest of her words.

Gideon listened hard, and by the end of the conversation thought she'd said something about having a try from the back of the hill, trying to get to the top of it from the other side.

"Looks like we're stuck here," he said to Lorna, trying to sound bright about it. Truth was, coming in from the back wasn't easy because the terrain over there was much like it was on this side. All mud and water, with more rain threatening to make it even worse. Not so many houses, though, which was the only spark of optimism at getting out of here. However it worked out, however they got to them—and they would, he absolutely knew that—there wasn't a damn thing he could for now except wait. And help Lorna deliver a couple of babies.

Lorna applied counter-pressure to Jussara's back to help relieve some of the pain. They'd been there an hour now, and the contractions were progressing. The poor woman was so uncomfortable...intermittently vomiting and drinking the juice Gideon was tying to force down her in order to keep her hydrated. Right now, it was simply about waiting. And the praying that the house wouldn't come down on them or that Gideon's crew would find a way in.

Zé was in the front room, playing with Max, who was more patient about it than any dog had a right to be. And over the course of Jussara's very broken English and Lorna's even more limited understanding of Brazilian Portuguese, she thought she'd figured out that Jussara's husband was actually down at base camp, helping in the rescue effort. Had he known his wife was in labor when he'd left her? She looked over at Gideon for a moment, then looked away.

"What?" he asked.

"Nothing."

"That wasn't a nothing look you just gave me."

"OK, I was wondering if Mr. Azevedo knew his wife was in labor when he left her?"

Instead of replying, Gideon glanced away.

"Look, I didn't mean to start something between us, but you asked."

"And right now you're thinking about how I left you. How I knew you were spotting that day and left anyway."

Actually, she hadn't been thinking that. Over the years, the memory had dissipated. She hadn't wanted to think about that time in her life, and for the most part she'd successfully blocked out the worst of the memories. "No," she whispered. "I wasn't."

He snapped his head around to glare at her. "I don't believe that! You divorced me because of it."

So here it was. The other shoe dropping, so to speak. She'd wondered when they would get around to this, had hoped they wouldn't, figured they would. "I divorced you for a lot of reasons, Gideon. For shutting me out, for never being home, for never really being with me when you were there, for hating my television job and always finding subtle ways to remind me…you not being there when I miscarried was only one of the many."

"The worst of them," he said, his voice going from defensive to sad. "And I'm so sorry, Lorna. For everything, but especially for not being with you that day. You don't know how many times I've…" He shut his eyes and shook his head. "I've hated myself for that."

"It wasn't anybody's fault," she said gently. "The doctor said I was fine, that you could go. Nobody could have predicted what happened…" Predicted the end of so many things. "You didn't know, Gideon. I know I said some awful things at the time, blamed you, accused of being glad you weren't going to be tied down, but I got counseling afterwards. Joined a support group. And the one thing I learned was that there isn't blame. A lot of angry and helpless feelings, often many irresponsible words, but no blame."

"You got help?"

"To get through it, I had to. Oh, I know there were other problems, but the miscarriage just became the most convenient one, the excuse I used to get rid of you, Gideon. I held it against you and blamed you and fixed on it until I couldn't function, when the truth was I felt like such a failure. Such a simple, natural thing, having a baby. And I couldn't do it."

He shook his head sadly. "God, we were all over the place, weren't we? Fighting against so many things, and none of them that mattered."

"We did have our share of problems.' She smiled at Jussara reassuringly. "And I think, for me, the worst was that I always felt like I was in second place with you, especially after I took the job with the television station. After that we never seemed to click like we had before. Then after I miscarried, I was just too tired to figure it out. Too hurt. Too broken-hearted. I think I'd convinced myself that having a baby would keep you with me more, make things right with us again, and when our baby…died, there just wasn't enough left in me that wanted to try and compete for your attention. I didn't think I could win."

"Oh, God, Lorna. You were never second place. But I thought I was. Or would be." He set Jussara's cup down after she'd finished drinking, then took a cloth from the warm water in a pot sitting on the table next to the bed. After wringing it out, he laid it over Jussara's belly. "I wanted our baby, Lorn. More than anything I've ever wanted in my life. At the time, I know you thought that I didn't, that I was relieved I wouldn't have to be tied down with family responsibilities. But I wanted our baby. I'd even bought…baby things."

She blinked in surprised. "You did? You never told me."

"Because by that time neither of was listening. We'd gone past the point of no return, and it wouldn't have made a difference."

"What?" she asked. "What had you bought?"

A sad smile touched his lips. "A stuffed bear for a girl, and a baseball mitt for a boy. I ran out and bought them the day you told me we were going to have a baby."

Suddenly, Lorna felt tears stinging at the back of her eyes. "I wish I could have seen them. Maybe it would have made things…better. Different."

"I kept them," he said. "I tried to throw them away a few times, but I couldn't. I thought…"

Jussara broke in with a load moan, followed by a gush of clear fluid. Instantly, Lorna took a look and, finally, the first baby was crowning. "It's on the way," she said, positioning herself for the delivery

Instinctively, Jussara, who'd been lying on her side, turned over and pushed herself up to her hands and knees.

"And I think she's ready to have at it," Gideon said, stepping back. "I don't guess I've ever seen…"

"On hands and knees?" Lorna laughed. "It's the natural way. Or squatting. Women were doing it long before anyone told them they needed a doctor present, and that a hard, flat table with stirrups was the proper way."

"Not my field of expertise," he said, forcing back a grimace as Jussara moaned again.

"It will be, after we get these babies into the world." With Jussara's shift in position, the contractions seemed to start coming harder and faster almost immediately, until finally the woman began to push.

"Damn," Gideon muttered, dampening another cloth and applying this one to Jussara's head. "Now I know why I didn't go into obstetrics."

Lorna laughed as she began the delivery. "And why men aren't the ones to have the babies." He would have been good at their childbirth, she thought. Or totally passed out on the floor and completely in everybody's way. "Look, this baby's going to come out pretty fast once it's started. Can you handle the cord?"

He nodded.

"The other one may come out pretty quickly, too. As best I can tell, it's turning into position and getting ready, so there's a good chance you'll be clamping the cord as the next one's crowning."

"Is it too late to postpone this until we can get her to the hospital?" he asked, sounding a bit winded.

"Take it up with Jussara," she said, laughing as she positioned herself to deliver the baby's head. As she did, a strong contraction hit the woman and she straightened her legs, pushing her bottom into the air. Then suddenly, baby! She came out easily and Gideon set about finishing the delivery as Lorna got ready for the next birth, which followed in only a few minutes. This time, a boy.

Two babies, big and healthy! And, blessedly, full term, judging by the size of them. That had been the one unknown factor in all this. She could handle a delivery, Gideon, as a surgeon, could have handled a Caesarean, if that had turned out to be needed. But the condition of the babies...the great big unknown, and the one fear she hadn't vocalized because it hit too close to losing her own baby. The Azevedo twins were big and healthy and fussing at the world already. As she finished cleaning up Jussara, Lorna glanced briefly over at Gideon, who was holding the little boy now, counting fingers and toes.

Rescue medicine was his element without a doubt. But so was this. He would have been a good father.

When mother and babies were finally settled in as best as they could be under the circumstances, Lorna went out into the other room and collapsed on the floor.

"You're amazing," Gideon said, coming out to join her. He slid to the floor next to her. "Her vital signs are good, I checked the twins and they're doing fine. Zé is in there with her now, and all's well with the Azevedo family. So, are you OK?"

"Fine. Tired, exhilarated, but fine. Except that we can't get out," Lorna said. "And the roof is creaking, and the side windows have busted out."

He looked across the room, and sure enough…"I'm going to go have a look around and see if there's any way to get us out."

She knew there wasn't, but she also knew Gideon had to try. "We should have talked about it years ago, Gideon. I should have talked about it when you wouldn't," she said, giving his hand a squeeze before he stood. "But I was so hurt by that time…Back then I wasn't the assertive, confident person who could speak up the way I do now and while you were shutting me out I let you do it."

"And I always assumed that going along on two separate tracks like we were worked out just fine. My parents are brilliant at it after all, and they were my examples, unfortunately."

"Well, if it's any consolation, after we split, I started a group for couples who have suffered a miscarriage. It's a time when you need to be closer, to heal, but so many people don't get through it. They push each other away, like we did."

"I'm proud of you," he whispered. "In so many ways, including what you do on television."

"Are you really?"

He nodded. "It was never the television program that was the threat, only I couldn't see it. All I could see was something I wanted so desperately being taken from me. I never considered that you weren't like my parents, that you wouldn't push me away, like they did. It was just some leftover feelings of one very hurt little boy coming through, and I'm sorry it happened. But I didn't know, Lorna. I didn't realize…"

She brushed back a tear streaking down her muddy face. "I'm proud of you, Gideon. Everything you've done… Being even a small part of something so important has helped me understand you in ways I never did before. Ways I should have."

"Not a small part, Lorna. Even though I've been hard on you, you've fit in here. But this has been a bad one, with Tom…" His voice cracked, and he cleared his throat. "There were a lot of things we should have talked about years ago. But sometimes, when you're going through it, you can't see things clearly enough to know what to do. I honestly had this picture in my head of the three of us living a normal life. You, me, baby. But all this…" He pointed to the mud that had oozed in through the window. "It's not normal life, is it? And it can't be. That's not who I am."

"Not who either of us are." From the other room, the cries of two babies caught their attention. "That's normal life, though," Lorna whispered. "No matter what else is going on here, that's truly normal life."

"Lorna, I…" The rest of Gideon's words were drowned out by the creaking roof overhead. It was beginning to give under the weight of the mud sliding down from up top. "We need to get everybody into the most secure area."

Lorna jumped up. "I'll drag the kitchen table into the doorway, and get everybody under it."

"No! That's a common misconception. Doorways and tables collapse, and if you're under them… Get everybody on the floor, right up against the bed. If the ceiling comes down, that's the best bet for safety…the spot next to a bed or sofa can provide a little empty air pocket."

Lorna nodded. This was why he was the best. Search and rescue—it was where he belonged. Not for the first time, her heart swelled with that knowledge. "Could I interview you about safety procedures for my television program some time?" she asked hesitantly, following Gideon to the front door. The last time she'd mentioned an interview, he'd gone all moody and snapped at her, and even though they'd cleared away so much of their personal debris, she still wasn't sure.

He turned around and gave her a quick kiss. "Name the date, and I'll be there."

Definitely a much better outcome than last time. Maybe things truly were turning around for them. Not simply wishful thinking any longer, but a real, solid base that could lead to a future. "You be careful out there, Gideon. I don't want anything to happen to you."

"When this is over Lorna, when we get back home…"

She pressed her index finger to his lips. "It'll keep until later," she said.

"Until later," he repeated, then dashed outside and forced the door shut behind him.

She would have gone to the window to watch, except the rain was pouring in, and what little view there might have been was obstructed by a large tree that had fallen and missed the house by mere inches. "I love you, Gideon," she whispered, then turned and ran to the bedroom.

CHAPTER ELEVEN

Jussara Azevedo waved farewell to Lorna as the volunteers carried her and her babies up the hill behind the house where the helicopter had found a little patch on which to set down. Little Zé tagged along behind, skipping playfully through the mud, completely oblivious to the fact that when the rains were over his home might be gone. To a child that age, those things didn't matter. Jussara was aware, though, because she carried her family pictures with her, along with a hand-made lace tablecloth from her grandmother. Nothing else, and she wasn't sad about it. Her children would soon be safe and nothing else mattered.

Max was being evacuated, too. Priscilla was leading him away because Gideon didn't want to put him at any more risk. In a while, when the first rescue was completed, the helicopter would return for them.

"Glad that's over," Gideon said, letting out a sigh of relief as he stepped back to appraise the structure. It was sound enough, and because the rains had diminished, along with the winds, the Azevedo family might turn out to be one of the lucky ones who had a house to return to. Damage, but not total destruction.

"Could we walk out?" Lorna asked. "The way we came in?"

"We could try, but we'd have to go an awful long way around, and nothing below here is stable enough yet. I'd rather wait."

His teams were already out on search, combing the debris in safer areas. By now the majority of the people who had lived here on the outskirts of Francisco do Monte were gone, and only those who remained to pick through what was left of their homes lingered behind. In such a short time the area had become like a ghost town…from so many people trying to get away to only a handful who'd chosen to stay. "What happens next?" she asked Gideon.

"Well, I'll keep the team here as long as the rains keep coming and the local authorities think we're needed, but we might move a little further north in a few days. There's another area of mudslides, larger overall area but with fewer houses, probably about fifty kilometers away. They've already got their rescue teams in place, but we may go in as the second responders if they need us. If they don't, when the rains quit and all our patients are sent to proper facilities, we all go home until next time."

"And you never know when next time will come." Lorna opened the door of the Azevedo house and went back inside, then sat down on the floor near where she'd spent an hour huddled next to the bed with two babies, one mother and a very anxious little boy. Not to mention a dog. "That's quite a way to live a life."

Gideon chuckled, sliding down to the floor next to her. Instinctively, he slid his arm around her shoulder, and she leaned into him immediately. "You get used to it. You keep everything ready to go and when the call comes in it's all organized. Maybe not by a regular schedule, but by the standards of what anybody who lives on call is used to. And it's not a bad life. Not traditional, not the way most people would choose to live. But it's good."

"Jason said you don't go by the rules. Gwen said the same thing. You force everybody else to do as you say, but you don't. Why, Gideon?"

"Gwen has a husband and a brand-new grandchild. Jason has Priscilla and two children. Brian has a companion. When I put them at extreme risk, I'm involving so many other people."

"So you put yourself at extreme risk because there's no one else involved?"

He shrugged. "I'm not reckless and, trust me, I don't have a death wish. But it's easier for me to do some of the things I wouldn't ask others to do. And I'm not being a reluctant hero or anything. Just practical."

"It's not practical putting yourself in the way of harm, Gideon."

"You sound like you'd almost be worried."

"Of course I'd be worried. I always was when we were married. Did you ever know that on the nights you were gone I didn't sleep? I paced the floor, stayed by the phone. It was awful, never knowing."

"I'm sorry," he said. "I didn't know."

"I always thought you should have, that you should simply know. I should have told you, Gideon. Maybe if you'd known…" Her voice broke, and she swallowed back a lump in her throat. "Anyway, when I miscarried, you'd already been shutting me out for months. It was like I lost the one thing I thought would be the bond that would keep us together. I just didn't want to deal with the pain, didn't want to see you walk away from me any more than you already had. So I walked away from you."

"We were quite a pair, weren't we? Both of us a mess of issues and conflicting lives. Me shutting you out, you not able to tell me how you felt."

"Both of us fighting rejection issues by rejecting each other." If only they'd talked then like they were talking now.

He pulled her even closer. "Do you realize how alike we are?"

"If you'd said that to me five years ago, I've have told you that you were crazy. But I think you're right. We do thrive on the edge more than most people do, don't we? You in your crazy life-style and me in mine."

"Crazy by whose definition?"

She laughed. "Would you take me on to do an occasional

rescue?" she asked, out of the blue. "After I've had some proper training? I'm going to make some changes in my life, and that's one I'd like to make." She'd been giving it thought for a while, not sure if she would actually take the big leap and ask.

"God, Lorna, that scares me."

"You mean the two of us together? Because we don't have to…"

"No that. But even the thought of you being in danger…"

"Priscilla and Jason survive that, and it works for them. I think it makes them even closer."

"But there's Dani and Tom…" He let out a weary sigh. "Lorna, I've thought about that day a thousand times since then, thought about how close you were to being there, to being the one who could have gone in to rescue the child. And you did go in. It scared the hell out of me, and I felt so damned helpless outside, holding onto the radio, waiting to hear something from you. Wondering if something bad was happening."

"The way I always felt when you left me at home. I want to do this, Gideon. I'm sure I can find another team, but I want to do it with you. I mean, when we were married I wasn't ready for it. But had we waited a few years before we met and married, maybe we'd be Jason and Priscilla, trooping off together and leaving the kiddies with their grandparents. Living on the edge of something normal, but not quite."

"Can't go back," Gideon said almost regretfully.

"And I'm not sure how to go forward." She twisted to look at him, and caught his intent gaze on her. "What are we going to do, Gideon?" she whispered.

"If I were to say yes, how could you fit it into your schedule? My people are on call twenty-four seven. We don't have the luxury of accepting or declining an assignment based on what else is going on in our lives. It's an all-or-nothing commitment.""

"And you don't think I can do all or nothing?" she snapped.

"Actually, I know you can. But that doesn't change the fact

that I'm developing these rather intrusive, protective feelings about you."

"Protective?" She laughed. "Care to tell me more?"

"No," he grumbled. "I don't care to tell you more."

"You know, Gideon, while I was sitting there on the floor with the Azevedo family, knowing that Jussara Azevedo knew she might never return to her home, it started me thinking about the important things in a person's life. When you get right down to it, nothing is as important as the people…the friends we make, the people we love. Everything Jussara had in her home might be gone, and all she wanted was her mother's tablecloth and the family photos. I want to join your team, Gideon. I want to be part of the work, and I can do that. If I move to Texas, they can transmit my daily medical segments to the network by satellite, and I may have to go to New York a couple days a week to tape my Sunday program, but that's easy enough."

"And your hospital work?"

"There are hospitals in Texas that would have me."

"Lorna, do you know what you're saying? That you're willing to fit your schedule around Global Response and, in a large way, around me?"

"I'm not your parents, Gideon," she said gently. "I'm not looking for a reason to leave. I want to be closer to you, and what I do won't get in the way."

"So, is this the two of us starting over? A new relationship? Marriage? "

"Maybe, if that's not being too presumptuous. Because I want to stay close to you, Gideon, however we work it out, and see what happens. We lost so much the first time because we weren't close enough…because neither of us truly let the other one know what we needed. I mean, it was like we both had our own little lives and we met in the middle occasionally. And that's not a marriage, not really. You were right, though, when you said we weren't ready, because we weren't. I hadn't found myself, Gideon, and you were just finding yourself, and that's what killed us. We were never together, emotionally. So, maybe I'm seeing this the wrong way, but I think you might want me here. Of course, maybe you don't want me here at all. And if that's the case, tell me now and we don't have to talk about this again."

"Dear God, Lorna. I want you here! I've looked for every excuse to push you away, tried hard to do it, tried hard to convince myself I'd be better off without you. But I never have been. Not once, in all these years because…I don't know how to put this into words." He drew in a ragged breath. "I've known for a long time that we weren't over. I didn't know how we would come together, didn't know why, didn't have a clue about an outcome. Would we be friends or lovers? Would we finally get through the past, the loss of our child…do it together as we couldn't before? Or would the old animosities still be there? I've had all these years to think about our next meeting, planning how it would happen, then there it was, yet I hadn't figured out anything at all. To be honest, it scared me, Lorna. I've never hated you. You needed something from me that I didn't know how to give because I was too busy expecting you to fit into my mold instead of working on a mold for the two of us. And now I know that you needed something from yourself that you didn't yet have, and I didn't support you in finding it." Gideon bent down and brushed a kiss to Lorna's muddy cheek, then one to her lips. "I'm glad you came here," he said on a deep sigh, pulling her head to his chest. "I'm sorry I didn't fight harder for us before."

Lorna laughed. "I should have, too, but I didn't know how hard marriage was. Happily-ever-after takes a lot of work!"

"We weren't all bad back then, though."

"You know, for the longest time all I could see was the bad, but lately it's not so clear as it was, and I'm beginning to remember more of the good…like our walks on the beach when we had a chance to get away, and how I used to love it when you'd read to me in bed."

"Romance novels," he said, turning up his nose in jest.

"With those happily-ever-after endings I'm just now coming to appreciate for what they take."

"Happily-ever-after in the days when we thought we'd have it," he said.

"But happily-ever-after beginnings are nice, too," she added, tilting her face to kiss Gideon. "Second beginnings and second chances." Just as their lips touched, though, the ceiling overhead shrieked an agonizing protest and they both looked up.

"If we want to get to that happily-ever-after second beginning, I think we'd better get the hell out of here!" he cried. Gideon jumped up and pulled Lorna up with him, then dragged her to the door, shoving her out ahead of him. By the time they'd both cleared the house by a few meters, the ceiling went crashing in. Lorna tried to pause for a look, but Gideon had a firm hold on her hand and kept pulling her down the hill with him. Running frantically, slipping and sliding in the mud and trying to keep themselves upright, once they came to a relatively flat spot, off to the side of what could be a glide path for the house, he dragged her into a clump of trees, where she collapsed to the ground. But he wouldn't let her stay down. Not even for a second. "We've got to keep going" he shouted breathlessly, as he turned back for a momentary appraisal, trying to figure out what next to do as the Azevedo house literally shimmied to the side, then buckled in on itself. "It's coming down," he said, pulling Lorna deeper into the little wooded thicket, thanking heaven they weren't tall straight palms.

The next time he turned around to take a look, the house was completely flattened, lost in the wash of mud coming down over top of it in a slow gush. "Can you climb?" Gideon asked, looking up the tree.

Without saying a word, Lorna spotted the sturdiest branch within her reach, jumped up and grabbed hold. Gideon immediately steadied her swinging body and helped lift her fully onto a branch. It was awkward, and she wasn't too steady. Once up, though, she balanced herself in a sitting position and grabbed hold of the trunk, hugging it like she'd never hugged anything in her entire life. And she kept her eyes squeezed shut for an eternity, holding her breath, for fear that even the slightest little jostle would send her plummeting to the ground below. But eventually her breath gave out and she was forced to draw in another. At that same time she opened her eyes to find Gideon, but he wasn't there. She looked down, blinked, looked down again. Then gingerly she twisted a little to the side, had a look over her shoulder, saw nothing!

Panic gripped her instantly, especially when, out of the corner of her eye, she could see the mud and all sorts of debris picking up intensity in its slide down the mountain. "Gideon," she whispered because nothing louder would come out. She'd thought he was coming up with her, and she actually ventured a look upwards to see if he was overhead, but he wasn't. "Gideon," she choked, this time a little louder.

This couldn't be happening! He'd made it. Gideon wouldn't have got himself caught in the muddy avalanche. Not Gideon! "Gideon, where are you?" she called again, now braving a louder shout. But he didn't answer, and all she could hear was the racket of the Azevedo house sliding its way downward.

Amazing, how loud it sounded. To her ears, it was screaming. "Gideon!" She finally mustered a decent shout as she gathered up the courage to make a full twist to the side and have a better look further down the wash. "Can you hear me?" She couldn't see him anywhere, not caught up and being carried along in it. But, then, she couldn't see much of anything.

"Gideon!" she finally screamed at the top of her lungs, panic clutching at her throat like bony fingers, threatening to rob her of her next breath. She had to find him. Get out of the tree and find him! "Gideon!" she screamed again. "Can you hear me?"

"Over here!" he shouted. "Lorna, I'm over here!"

It took her a moment to find him, but when she did he was well on his way up another tree. For that brief instant she went numb with relief. So many horrible images had flashed through her mind in those few seconds when she'd thought she'd lost him. Awful images about never seeing him again, about a new beginning that would never happen, about spending the rest of her life without the man she loved. And she did love Gideon. Desperately.

"Didn't have to time to wait until you got situated," he called. "Had to find my own tree."

"Are we safe?" she managed, swiping back the tears starting to stream down her face. Not tears of fright, though. Tears of happiness. Gideon was alive and well, and nothing else in this world mattered.

"The debris isn't large enough to knock down the trees, and the mud's not going to uproot them. So we're fine. But we may be in for a long wait up here."

Didn't matter. None of it did. She could sit in the tree for hours, or days, if that's what it took to be with him when they finally got down. Yes, they *were* fine. He'd said it, and she trusted him. They were absolutely fine, Gideon up his tree and she up hers. "So, what we were talking about before?" she shouted, deciding she may as well make the best of their situation since there was no telling when they'd have time to sit down and have a heart to heart again. "About me moving to Texas…" And starting a whole new life with him.

"It won't be easy, Lorna."

"I don't need easy. I know what I'm getting and I'm ready for it." Ready like she'd never been in her life.

"Won't be traditional either."

"Don't need traditional." All she needed was Gideon. If he would have her, the rest would work itself out in ways that would matter only to them. "And we've got to talk, Gideon. No matter what else, we've got to talk. Tell each other how we feel, never shut each other out again. Every day, every night. And I want you to train me to go out on rescues, then trust your training—and trust me—that I'll be good at it. I don't want you hovering over me all the time, worrying. And trying to protect me."

"Got to protect you, Lorna. That's part of the package. But I won't hover…too much. And I want to come with you when you tape your shows to see what you do."

A little hovering and protecting wasn't bad. That's what husbands and wives did. "Are you sure? That's going to mean New York."

"I can do New York when I'm not on call. As long as I'm doing it with you. So, do you need a house?" he called. "Or would you be OK living in the warehouse with me?"

"A warehouse is good." A tent pitched with Gideon would be dandy. A tree house would be fine, too, as long as she was with Gideon.

"So would it be appropriate now for me to tell you that I love you, and that I never stopped?" he shouted. "Or would you rather wait until we can go someplace romantic, have candlelight and champagne, and soft music in the background?"

She thought about the first time he'd told her he loved her. It had been by candlelight, and they had had champagne and soft music in the background. She'd thought that was the most romantic, magical moment of her life. But she'd been wrong. This was. They were two crazies sitting in two trees, they were covered with mud, planning a life that no rational person would ever think could work, and to her this was the most romantic, most magical moment of her life. "It would be appropriate," she called over to him.

"Good, because I don't want to wait, Lorna. I don't want to wait to tell you that I love you, and I don't want to wait to ask you to marry me again."

And she didn't want to wait either. "I love you too," she cried, as the rescue helicopter lifted up over the top of the hill and hovered above. "And I'll marry you!"

"What?" he shouted. But she couldn't hear over the whir of the rotor.

"Yes! I'll marry you," she shouted, fully realizing her words would never make it to Gideon's ears. But they didn't have to. From the look on his face, they'd made it to his heart.

Gideon rolled over in bed and laid his hand across Lorna's belly. This was their third lazy day in São Paulo, the city that had become their favorite place in the world. They'd been there three times over the months, helping Ana Flavia get ready for her move to Texas with them as she'd become like a second mother to them both. She was learning their language, as they were hers. And what they'd learnt was that her son lived in Chicago, her daughter in Florida. So Ana Flavia was excited to be moving closer to her own family, and closer to her new family, where she was going to be a second grandmother and caregiver for Ana Merrill, her soon-to-be namesake. In fact, the day after tomorrow, when Lorna and Gideon returned to Houston, they would be escorting Ana Flavia to her new home, a nice little flat they'd fixed for her right in their warehouse.

"Baby's kicking like a real soccer player this morning," he said.

"She's had enough traveling around as part of my luggage. I think she's ready to get out and see the world on her own." Lorna had gotten pregnant that night in São Paulo. No, it hadn't been her time of the month to conceive, but she and Gideon both looked on it as one of those miracles that were meant to be. The Fates giving them a reason to be together if they hadn't worked it out for themselves. Now, nearly eight months later, Gideon's stuffed animal from years ago sat in the crib in the room they'd prepared for their baby, along with the baseball mitt in case little Ana had a preference for sports.

"Well, I'm just as ready as she is," he said, pulling down the bed sheet to stare at Lorna's swollen belly. He'd done that a lot lately. And, yes, he did protect and hover, but she adored it. Wouldn't have it any other way.

Life was working out beautifully. Her daily televisions segments by satellite were coming along nicely, most done in Houston now but some done by remote in the rescue field. Her audiences actually loved that, seeing her out with Gideon, doing something worthy. It added a new depth to her advice. Also, her trips back to New York to film her Sunday television show were easy, even though she missed Gideon terribly when she was gone. Until just a few weeks ago she'd gone out on about half of Gideon's responses as an active medic, and even now, when she wasn't so active, she still tagged along just so she wouldn't have to be separated from him. Although, admittedly, she'd given up those bed rolls on the wooden floors in the tent and now toted along a cushy air mattress.

She'd never taken up practice in a hospital, though. Instead, she'd devoted herself to being a one-woman ambassador for Gideon's emergency preparedness program for children, and traveled about as often as she could, teaching and handing out backpacks. The program was a success, and thanks to a little television push the demand for more was greater than anything they'd ever anticipated.

And she had her rescue work, the real hands-on care she needed to do. Later, when little Ana was part of the family, Ana Flavia would be the one to care for her when Lorna and Gideon went off on a rescue. But the one condition would always be that their daughter came first, no matter what. A child as wanted as she was would never feel unwanted when they went off, and they would devote their lives to making her secure in that.

Also, no matter where Lorna went, her rescue dog in training, Maisey, went with her. Oh, Max was a little put out at first, not being the only dog. But he got over it. And he still slept with Gideon, only on the floor next to the bed, as Lorna now had Max's spot, curled up next to Gideon.

It was one big, happy family with Jason and Priscilla and their kiddies as extended family, and Ana Flavia soon to be the new grandmother, two dogs, little Ana on the way, and a whole troop of rescue volunteers weaving in and out all the time. Big, happy, not traditional. Everything Lorna had ever wanted and more than she ever thought she'd have.

"You know what I'd like to do?" she said lazily, stretching and wiggling her toes.

"What?" Gideon asked, smiling.

"Have you give me a nice foot rub."

"Give you a foot rub? What's in it for me?"

"The satisfaction of knowing you have a very contented wife."

"Is she contented?" Gideon asked, reaching over to give her belly another rub. "Really contented?"

More than she'd ever known she could be. "She is. But is he?"

Instead of answering, he pulled her over to him and kissed her lightly on the lips, then kissed her on the belly. "Contented, and getting even more contented by the day."

"Then skip the foot rub," she said, wiggling herself into a comfortable position in his arms. "Let's just stay here in bed like we are. *All day*. We'll call out for food. You can read me another romance novel. We can listen to soft music…something with a nice Brazilian flavor. We can put on those sunglasses and bandanas I bought from that street vendor and…"

"No bandanas," he said, seeking out her lips.

"No bandanas," she whispered, tilting her face to his.

MILLS & BOON®

Live the emotion

MARCH 2007 HARDBACK TITLES

ROMANCE™

The Billionaire's Scandalous Marriage *Emma Darcy*
978 0 263 19588 0
The Desert King's Virgin Bride *Sharon Kendrick*
978 0 263 19589 7
Aristides' Convenient Wife *Jacqueline Baird* 978 0 263 19590 3
The Pregnancy Affair *Anne Mather* 978 0 263 19591 0
Bought for Her Baby *Melanie Milburne* 978 0 263 19592 7
The Australian's Housekeeper Bride *Lindsay Armstrong*
978 0 263 19593 4
The Brazilian's Blackmail Bargain *Abby Green* 978 0 263 19594 1
The Greek Millionaire's Mistress *Catherine Spencer*
978 0 263 19595 8
The Sheriff's Pregnant Wife *Patricia Thayer* 978 0 263 19596 5
The Prince's Outback Bride *Marion Lennox* 978 0 263 19597 2
The Secret Life of Lady Gabriella *Liz Fielding* 978 0 263 19598 9
Back to Mr & Mrs *Shirley Jump* 978 0 263 19599 6
Memo: Marry Me? *Jennie Adams* 978 0 263 19600 9
Hired by the Cowboy *Donna Alward* 978 0 263 19601 6
Dr Constantine's Bride *Jennifer Taylor* 978 0 263 19602 3
Emergency at Riverside Hospital *Joanna Neil* 978 0 263 19603 0

HISTORICAL ROMANCE™

The Wicked Earl *Margaret McPhee* 978 0 263 19754 9
Working Man, Society Bride *Mary Nichols* 978 0 263 19755 6
Traitor or Temptress *Helen Dickson* 978 0 263 19756 3

MEDICAL ROMANCE™

A Bride for Glenmore *Sarah Morgan* 978 0 263 19792 1
A Marriage Meant To Be *Josie Metcalfe* 978 0 263 19793 8
His Runaway Nurse *Meredith Webber* 978 0 263 19794 5
The Rescue Doctor's Baby Miracle *Dianne Drake*
978 0 263 19795 2

MILLS & BOON®

0207 Gen Std LP

Live the emotion

MARCH 2007 LARGE PRINT TITLES

ROMANCE™

Purchased for Revenge *Julia James*	978 0 263 19431 9
The Playboy Boss's Chosen Bride *Emma Darcy*	
	978 0 263 19432 6
Hollywood Husband, Contract Wife *Jane Porter*	
	978 0 263 19433 3
Bedded by the Desert King *Susan Stephens*	978 0 263 19434 0
Her Christmas Wedding Wish *Judy Christenberry*	
	978 0 263 19435 7
Married Under the Mistletoe *Linda Goodnight*	978 0 263 19436 4
Snowbound Reunion *Barbara McMahon*	978 0 263 19437 1
The Tycoon's Instant Family *Caroline Anderson*	
	978 0 263 19438 8

HISTORICAL ROMANCE™

A Lady of Rare Quality *Anne Ashley*	978 0 263 19385 5
Talk of the Ton *Mary Nichols*	978 0 263 19386 2
The Norman's Bride *Terri Brisbin*	978 0 263 19387 9

MEDICAL ROMANCE™

Caring for His Child *Amy Andrews*	978 0 263 19339 8
The Surgeon's Special Gift *Fiona McArthur*	978 0 263 19340 4
A Doctor Beyond Compare *Melanie Milburne*	978 0 263 19341 1
Rescued By Marriage *Dianne Drake*	978 0 263 19342 8
The Nurse's Longed-For Family *Fiona Lowe*	978 0 263 19535 4
Her Baby's Secret Father *Lynne Marshall*	978 0 263 19536 1

0307 Gen Std HB

MILLS & BOON®

Live the emotion

APRIL 2007 HARDBACK TITLES

ROMANCE™

The Ruthless Marriage Proposal *Miranda Lee* 978 0 263 19604 7
Bought for the Greek's Bed *Julia James* 978 0 263 19605 4
The Greek Tycoon's Virgin Mistress *Chantelle Shaw*
978 0 263 19606 1
The Sicilian's Red-Hot Revenge *Kate Walker* 978 0 263 19607 8
The Italian Prince's Pregnant Bride *Sandra Marton*
978 0 263 19608 5
Kept by the Spanish Billionaire *Cathy Williams* 978 0 263 19609 2
The Kristallis Baby *Natalie Rivers* 978 0 263 19610 8
Mediterranean Boss, Convenient Mistress *Kathryn Ross*
978 0 263 19611 5
A Mother for the Tycoon's Child *Patricia Thayer*
978 0 263 19612 2
The Boss and His Secretary *Jessica Steele* 978 0 263 19613 9
Billionaire on her Doorstep *Ally Blake* 978 0 263 19614 6
Married by Morning *Shirley Jump* 978 0 263 19615 3
Princess Australia *Nicola Marsh* 978 0 263 19616 0
The Sheikh's Contract Bride *Teresa Southwick* 978 0 263 19617 7
The Surgeon and the Single Mum *Lucy Clark* 978 0 263 19618 4
The Surgeon's Longed-For Bride *Emily Forbes* 978 0 263 19619 1

HISTORICAL ROMANCE™

A Scoundrel of Consequence *Helen Dickson* 978 0 263 19757 0
An Innocent Courtesan *Elizabeth Beacon* 978 0 263 19758 7
The King's Champion *Catherine March* 978 0 263 19759 4

MEDICAL ROMANCE™

Single Father, Wife Needed *Sarah Morgan* 978 0 263 19796 9
The Italian Doctor's Perfect Family *Alison Roberts*
978 0 263 19797 6
A Baby of Their Own *Gill Sanderson* 978 0 263 19798 3
His Very Special Nurse *Margaret McDonagh*
978 0 263 19799 0

MILLS & BOON®

Live the emotion

0307 Gen Std LP

APRIL 2007 LARGE PRINT TITLES

ROMANCE™

The Christmas Bride *Penny Jordan*	978 0 263 19439 6
Reluctant Mistress, Blackmailed Wife *Lynne Graham*	
	978 0 263 19440 X
At the Greek Tycoon's Pleasure *Cathy Williams*	978 0 263 19441 8
The Virgin's Price *Melanie Milburne*	978 0 263 19442 6
The Bride of Montefalco *Rebecca Winters*	978 0 263 19443 4
Crazy about the Boss *Teresa Southwick*	978 0 263 19444 2
Claiming the Cattleman's Heart *Barbara Hannay*	
	978 0 263 19445 0
Blind-Date Marriage *Fiona Harper*	978 0 263 19446 9

HISTORICAL ROMANCE™

An Improper Companion *Anne Herries*	978 0 263 19388 8
The Viscount *Lyn Stone*	978 0 263 19389 6
The Vagabond Duchess *Claire Thornton*	978 0 263 19390 X

MEDICAL ROMANCE™

Rescue at Cradle Lake *Marion Lennox*	978 0 263 19343 8
A Night to Remember *Jennifer Taylor*	978 0 263 19344 6
The Doctors' New-Found Family *Laura MacDonald*	
	978 0 263 19345 4
Her Very Special Consultant *Joanna Neil*	978 0 263 19346 2
A Surgeon, A Midwife: A Family *Gill Sanderson*	978 0 263 19537 6
The Italian Doctor's Bride *Margaret McDonagh*	978 0 263 19538 4